"I've always liked rooting for the underdog...

"Looks like that's what both of us are." His wry-looking grin sent her thoughts in the wrong direction. His smiles were more disarming by the day.

"That's the truth." He folded one arm over the other as he leaned in again.

Worse, he stared straight into her eyes. She couldn't look away. Not liking him more than she already did was very serious business now that she'd be staying at the ranch full-time.

"I should put my clothes up." She scooted her chair back.

"Yeah." He stood.

"Thanks for helping me get everything upstairs."

"You're welcome. Good night."

"Good night. I'll do my best not to see you tomorrow, fellow underdog."

"Yeah. I'll do my best, too." He headed for the door.

She forced herself not to see him out. Not to think about looking at the stars with him. He wouldn't think about doing such a thing with her, would he?

Betty Woods writes encouraging stories for a discouraging world. She and her husband share their Texas home with a spoiled Chihuahua. One of her favorite pastimes is roaming through Texas towns and countryside sights. Her ideas and inspiration for a new story often come from those adventures. Being with family is one of her passions, especially spending time with her grandchildren. You can find out more at bettywoodsbooks.com or on Facebook.

Books by Betty Woods

Love Inspired

A Mother for His Son

Visit the Author Profile page at LoveInspired.com.

A Mother
for His Son

Betty Woods

LOVE INSPIRED
INSPIRATIONAL ROMANCE

LOVE INSPIRED®
INSPIRATIONAL ROMANCE

Recycling programs
for this product may
not exist in your area.

ISBN-13: 978-1-335-75932-0

A Mother for His Son

Love Inspired
22 Adelaide St. West, 41st Floor
Toronto, Ontario M5H 4E3, Canada
www.LoveInspired.com

Printed in U.S.A.

The Lord is my shepherd; I shall not want.
He maketh me to lie down in green pastures:
he leadeth me beside the still waters.
—*Psalm* 23:1–2

My book is dedicated to my wonderful family. You're all a blessing beyond what mere words can say.

To my wonderful husband, Craig,
my number one fan and my inspiration.

To Carlee and C.J., my precious inspirations
for Gabe's ladybug adventures with Rachel.

To my real aunt Connie and aunt Sharon.
Aunt Connie, you wanted to be in a book.
You got your wish!

Chapter One

Rachel Landry halted under the welcome shade of a huge pecan tree in front of the little church where she was supposed to meet her grandmother. She reread the text from Granna. The budget committee meeting was taking longer than planned. So Rachel had at least thirty minutes to kill before she and Granna could go grocery shopping.

In thirty minutes, she could walk across a big part of the town of Sunrise. Which was why she'd left her car at Granna's house and hiked the mile or so to the church. A quick tour of the Texas Hill Country town might be a good idea. She'd been so busy the last couple of years that she'd spent precious little time here. Re-learning where everything was might come in handy if she needed to run errands for her grandmother while she was here.

Shading her eyes from the glare of the evening sun, she glanced at the historical marker outside the church door. A lot of the downtown buildings here had markers or plaques telling their stories dating back as far as the 1870s. She turned to the east. Better to have the too-warm September sun heating her back than shining in her eyes as she walked.

By the time she'd gone a block from the church, she'd passed by a half dozen plaques proudly put up by the Chamber of Commerce. She paused in front of the library, housed in an old store built in 1885. Her once-hectic life had left no time for reading. She couldn't remember when she'd read an actual paperback instead of an ebook.

As she reached for the library door, it swung open in her face. A long-legged man dressed in jeans, boots and Western hat charged outside as he stared at his cell phone. She jumped back just in time to keep from being knocked to the sidewalk.

"Sorry. I wasn't paying attention to where I was going. Are you okay?" His wide-eyed stare signaled he was just as shocked at what he'd nearly done as she was.

"I'm fine. I'm used to dodging people with cell phones in Dallas all the time. Just never a cowboy before."

His sheepish-looking grin lit up his warm brown eyes. "Right, since 'Dallas is where the East peters out.'"

She shrugged. "Maybe. I never thought about it."

He laughed. "It's according to Will Rogers. And 'Fort Worth is where the West begins.'"

"Okay…" She wasn't sure where this conversation was headed. "But we're in Sunrise."

"True, but we're about a two-and-a-half-hour drive southwest from Fort Worth, so we're the West here."

"Oh."

"I'm Mac Greer, local rancher, who usually doesn't almost knock someone down."

"Rachel Landry." She couldn't help but return his infectious smile, especially since his wry humor appeared to signal he wasn't only concerned about himself.

"Miss Connie's granddaughter?" He swiped at a lock of brown hair threatening to fall into his eyes.

Rachel nodded.

"She's told everyone in and out of town you were coming to help her."

"For a few weeks." Best to let him know she wouldn't be here long.

She'd come to help Granna, not hunt for a new boyfriend—or worse, a husband. *Where'd that come from?* This man's grin didn't look at all flirtatious. He had yet to take in more than her face. Which was great. She'd come to Sunrise temporarily to help Granna. Period.

"Miss Connie's been bragging on you since the day she found out you were coming." Mac's words made for a needed interruption.

Any further thoughts on why she'd come to Sunrise would only bring back the depression she'd clawed her way out of. Two weeks of living in her pajamas and never leaving her apartment hadn't solved a single one of her problems. It had only magnified them and made them worse.

"I'm happy to be here." In more ways than one.

Just then, his phone chimed. "Sorry to be rude, but I'm running late."

Tipping his hat, he hurried off to his pickup. Much better than sticking around to say something else as inane as he'd just said. Introducing himself as a local rancher and all the trite stuff about East vs. West. Classy. Good thing he wasn't trying to impress Miss Connie's granddaughter. Her or any other woman. Those days were long gone after the way his wife deserted him and their son. So why had he thrown any kind of lines at Rachel Landry? She hadn't looked overly interested in him, which was fine. He had no interest of any kind in her.

Still, he couldn't remember the last time a woman had caught his attention the way Rachel Landry had. He couldn't come up with any kind of valid reason. He'd almost knocked her down, not vice versa. If one look in those friendly green eyes did this to him, he'd better be on guard.

He needed to think about why. He drove toward the edge of town. Toward his favorite open country, where he truly belonged. Running the family ranch short-handed was tough. But that was better than anything he'd ever found in town. The farther away he got, the more he relaxed his relaxed on the steering wheel.

He should have resigned from the library board today. Volunteering had sounded great until the others changed their minds about the number of in person meetings needed. He couldn't check fences by teleconference.

His view of the open road—with its mesquite and juniper trees—helped him relax. Home was only a few minutes away.

Rachel watched the rancher rush off to wherever he was late going to.

The rancher definitely wasn't rude. She couldn't recall any man ever tipping his hat to her. After, all, Sunrise was worlds away from Dallas.

Different wasn't always bad. It could be good. She walked inside the small library, taking in a refreshing breath of the cooler air. Air-conditioning was still a necessity for a Texas September. Bright signs on the bookshelves, colorful child-size plastic chairs and tables scattered around made for a welcoming place. A sign by the nearby stairs read Reference and Adult Fiction, with an arrow pointing up.

The old wooden steps creaked under her sandals. Less than twenty minutes later, she left holding the first book she'd checked out in years. The librarian had also heard Rachel was coming to visit and happily signed her up for a library card.

The joys of a small town where everyone knew everybody. Her father had once said if someone sneezed in Sunrise, someone else would hear about it and come running with a tissue. Since she had yet to come across a single person who didn't know she was coming, her father had to be right.

Checking her watch, she quickened her pace. Granna should be through with her meeting soon, since it was a little after four o'clock.

Cane in hand, her petite, silver-haired grandmother stepped outside not long after Rachel got back to the church. Lively green eyes brightened the instant she caught sight of Rachel. "I'm sorry to make you wait."

Rachel held up the library book. "No problem. I found something to do."

She purposely didn't mention the cowboy she'd almost literally run into. Granna, aka Mrs. Constance Mae Landry, had a legendary reputation as a perpetual matchmaker in their family. Since so many people already knew about Rachel coming here, Granna's reputation was probably legendary in the entire little town of Sunrise and beyond, too.

Mac had been more interested in his phone than her. Which was perfect. Her disaster of a relationship with Dillon had left her in no mood to think about romance now. If ever again. She doubted many people had lost a fiancé and a job all in one day the way she had.

"I had no idea I'd run this late. Let's go out for supper. We can come back for groceries tomorrow." Granna's words brought Rachel's musings back to her more pleasant here and now.

Supper this early? She kept her thoughts to herself. Grabbing lunch at three had happened so often at her last job it had almost become normal. But if Granna wanted to eat now, then supper would be at four.

"Let's go to the Morning Glory Café. I'm hungry for fried catfish and hush puppies." Granna handed the car keys to Rachel. "I'm tired. You drive."

The very reason Rachel had come. Not that she wanted Granna to still tire so easily after her hip surgery this spring. But Granna wanted Rachel to do something for her that she'd been doing herself for years. A good sign the family's plan should work. As soon as her grandmother realized she needed to hire someone to help her a few days a week, Rachel could go back to Dallas, where she belonged.

Back to what, she didn't know, not after the way her life had fallen apart a couple of weeks ago.

She parked Granna's faded green Camry in front of the café. The light yellow sign with blue morning glories twining around the edges had hung in the plate-glass window ever since she'd come here as a kid.

Since they were so early, the place was fairly empty, and they soon sat at a corner table. Rachel studied the menu. Blackened salmon, chicken Florentine and stuffed pork chops along with the usual Texas delicacies of chicken-fried steak and fried catfish.

"This is quite a variety for a small café." She looked over at Granna, who hadn't even opened her menu.

"Everything in here is wonderful. Lance, the owner, trained as a chef in Dallas, same as you." Her eyes twinkled. She must really be looking forward to the fried catfish.

"That explains the eclectic menu, then."

About the time Granna started to take a bite of her second catfish filet, a blond-haired thirty-something year old man came over to their table. "Good evening, ladies. How is everything?"

"Delicious as usual." Granna's fork halted midair over her plate. "Lance, this is my granddaughter, Rachel."

"It's a pleasure. Miss Connie has told everyone about you."

Rachel finished chewing the bite of green beans she'd just popped into her mouth. "Thank you."

"Rachel is a chef, too. She got excellent reviews in Dallas at the restaurant where she worked." Granna glowed with pride.

"I hope you like our simple home-style cooking here." His blue eyes searched her face as if waiting for her answer.

"Nothing wrong with simple. My chicken is cooked perfectly." Rachel picked up her tea glass.

"Good. I'd love to show you our kitchen after you're through eating."

She hoped his broad smile aimed solely at her was because he enjoyed talking to another chef. But she hadn't planned on a personal tour of anyone's kitchen today. Especially since she wasn't sure she'd ever cook professionally again. Still, she couldn't be rude, could she?

"We could do that. Granna's a wonderful cook and would enjoy a behind-the-scenes look, too. Right?" Rachel looked across the table at her grandmother.

No matter how nice Lance seemed to be, she didn't want to do a solo tour with a man who wasn't wearing a wedding ring. And whom Granna looked much too happy to see giving Rachel so much attention.

Granna shook her head. "I'm no chef. I don't need to come along."

"You were one of my biggest encouragers to go to culinary school. I wouldn't think of you not sharing something so fun with me."

"Well…okay, sugar. As long as I won't be in the way."

"You could never be in the way." Rachel refocused her attention on Lance, who still looked very hopeful about his offer. "We'll be happy to see your kitchen after dessert."

"After dessert, then." He grinned before walking toward the next table.

A short time later, they were in the kitchen. Rachel silently congratulated herself for including Granna in Lance's tour. Her alert grandmother took it all in, even asking a couple of good questions. Rachel made a few business-type comments, and they were done. Such a perfect way to avoid an uncomfortable encounter that brought back memories of Dallas she didn't want to deal with now.

Granna was uncharacteristically quiet on the short drive home. Without saying a word, she got out of the car and went inside, leaving Rachel to park the car in the garage alone. Her sharp grandmother had probably seen through Rachel's true reason for including her in the kitchen tour.

The good news was that Lance had been more interested in showing off his new oven than he'd been in Rachel. The only questions he'd asked her were about where she'd worked in Dallas. She'd dodged the questions as best she could.

No TV show blared as Rachel made her way to the living room. She was the one who liked quiet. Granna usually turned on the TV or radio as soon as she got home.

"Thank you for including me in looking at the kitchen tonight. I enjoyed seeing how they cook everything."

"You're welcome. I thought you'd like that." Rachel sat on the couch next to her grandmother.

Granna's smile faded as she looked into Rachel's

eyes. "That was quite a performance in the café. Lance had no intention of including me when he showed off his kitchen. Why was I the one to notice that instead of you?"

Because she wasn't interested in any man. But she knew better than to mention such thoughts to anyone in her family again. Mom and Dad hadn't understood her when she'd told them she was through with men after her second bad relationship. Her matchmaking grandmother for sure wouldn't understand.

"He's friendly, but I'm here to see you. Plus, I'll be going back to Dallas in a few weeks."

Granna nodded, giving Rachel some hope that her grandmother would remember she wouldn't be here very long.

"Maybe you can find a way to show me your kitchen after you find your next job."

"I don't know…"

She couldn't finish the rest of her sentence when she had no idea what her next job might be. No idea how to make the hurt go away every time she thought about her uncertain future or her painful past. What she knew for certain was she wouldn't repeat the mistakes she'd made.

"What don't you know, sugar?"

Granna's sympathetic tone caused Rachel's eyes to well up. She blinked away the moisture. The crying jags during the first two weeks after she'd lost both her dream job and fiancé, had been more than enough time for tears. She was past that.

"Pretty much everything." She sighed. "Maybe going to culinary school was a mistake."

"What? No. How can you say that?" Granna patted Rachel's arm.

"Everything's turned out so wrong."

"Oh, sugar." Granna wrapped her up in a hug. "Dillon's the one who did everything wrong. Not you."

Rachel pulled away enough to see her grandmother's face. "How could I have been so blind? So gullible? Why couldn't I see through him?"

"Loving someone means trusting them, not looking to find fault with them. Dillon betrayed your trust. He betrayed *you*."

Closing her eyes, she swallowed away the threatening tears. "Every word you said is true. But it still hurts so bad."

"The Lord sent you here so we could help each other, sugar." Granna patted her cheek.

Rachel took a deep breath as she looked into her grandmother's eyes, filled with love. "Maybe."

Granna released Rachel to look straight at her. "Not all men are like that one. God has someone much better just for you. You'll see."

"I was so wrong about what I thought I saw in him. What if I make a mistake like that with someone else?"

"Have you listened to how many times you used the word *I*?"

Rachel shook her head.

"Never get so busy you don't ask God to show you what He wants you to do or who He wants for you. Understand, sugar?"

"I do."

She really did. But being sure she truly understood God's direction was so much harder than talking about it. Which was why loving another man, risking misjudging his true motives, was out of the question.

Mac hurried toward the foyer at the back of the worship center with barely any time left before Bible study began. Since ranching was such a solitary job, he liked to talk to people on Sundays. Especially with his parents temporarily in Fort Worth while his mother recuperated from a badly broken leg. But Gabe hadn't been in any kind of rush this morning. Some days speeding up his five-year-old son could be like trying to make a turtle move as fast as a runaway bull.

Stepping inside, he paused to see who was here. The sanctuary held about forty to fifty people. It was a small church, where everybody knew everybody. Aunt Sharon stood in the foyer not far from the table with the coffee and doughnuts, talking with a small group that included Miss Connie and her granddaughter. He could grab something quick and go talk to his best friend, Les Tucker.

After his quick run-in with Rachel a couple of days ago, he hadn't been able to get her out of his mind. He kept remembering her honey-colored hair, her pleasant smile and her kind words in spite of how he'd almost knocked her to the sidewalk.

Even if he was in the market for a relationship with a woman again—which he wasn't—he'd never pick one from Dallas. She'd be here in town a little while, then go back where she belonged. Which was nowhere near where he wanted to be.

"Mac, you have to meet Rachel." Aunt Sharon looked straight at him before he could snag a doughnut and escape.

He forced one boot in front of the other. If his aunt wanted to introduce him to Rachel, the woman must not have mentioned their quick encounter from Friday. Point for Rachel. Maybe he'd so unimpressed her that she'd forgotten him.

"Mac, this is my granddaughter, Rachel Landry. Rachel, Mac Greer." Miss Connie grinned up at him from her chair.

"Nice to meet you, Rachel."

The green eyes he shouldn't remember sparkled in his direction. So she *did* remember him. "Nice to meet you, too."

"I haven't got my coffee yet. Anyone else want another cup?" He bit into his doughnut while waiting for a response.

"Thanks but I'm good." Harry McIntire, the town's CPA, spoke up. The others shook their heads.

Mac walked the three feet to the coffeepot, glad for a good excuse to put some space between himself and Rachel. She looked too good in her light green skirt and flowered top. The last time a woman had caught his eye so quickly had turned out so badly. His ex, Alicia, had tired of ranching, then deserted him and their infant son. No one would ever abandon him or Gabe again.

Miss Connie was finishing off her chocolate-iced doughnut when he rejoined his aunt's circle of friends.

"I did tell you Rachel is a chef, didn't I? These doughnuts don't compare to the chocolate cream pie Rachel fixed last night."

"Mac would agree with you, since that's his favorite dessert." Aunt Sharon grinned in his direction.

Glad he still had coffee to polish off so he didn't have to talk, Mac ignored her. He didn't want to know why his aunt was so quick to mention how much he liked chocolate cream pie. Unless she was hoping to draw attention to him? Lately she'd gone from hinting to outright insisting Mac should try dating again.

A few people moved toward the worship center. Rachel looked down to check her watch. Good. Only a few more seconds he'd have to keep reminding himself not to look at her.

"Granna, do you have a favorite pew for Bible study?"

"If I didn't sit on the second pew on the piano side, the whole church would think I'd lost my mind."

"Want to start that way?"

Miss Connie dabbed her mouth with her napkin. "I guess we should."

Aunt Sharon and Harry looked toward the worship center.

"We should go in, too." Harry refocused his attention on Aunt Sharon.

We? When had this happened?

"Are you about through with your coffee?" His aunt glanced at the paper cup in Mac's hand.

"Almost, but go on. I won't get lost."

The pair walked off side by side. Apparently Harry had had more in mind than good client service when he'd started bringing every financial paper to the ranch instead of emailing or faxing things the last few weeks. Aunt Sharon had been doing other things since coming for a visit in June and staying to help Mac with Gabe while his parents were gone.

He took his time finishing his coffee. Enough time that he was one of the last people to walk into the worship center. The back pew was still empty. Good. He didn't want to sit anywhere near Miss Connie and Rachel. Or his aunt and Harry, who had seated themselves in the pew behind the Landry ladies.

The Bible study teacher, Ken Mills, welcomed everyone. "Miss Connie, looks like your special visitor came. Would you like to introduce her?"

"My granddaughter, Rachel, is here to help me for a while."

"Welcome to Sunrise, Rachel. We're glad you're here." Ken then asked for prayer requests.

"Please keep praying for my mom. The surgery to repair her broken leg went well, but she can't start rehab for a few more weeks." Mac spoke loud enough so that his voice carried to the front.

Ken wrote the name Caroline Greer on the dry-erase board perched on an easel. "Tell her we're all praying for her."

"I will."

A few minutes later, Ken started the lesson. His personal faith shone through his observations on Psalm 23. Maybe one day Mac could be half the man of faith Ken was.

When the service began, the pastor's sermon about

resting in the Lord spoke to him, too. Running the ranch without Dad's help gave him precious little rest. That wouldn't change anytime soon. His parents had to stay in Fort Worth to get the specialized rehab Mom needed after tripping over a tree root and badly breaking her leg. But as Pastor Leon said, resting in God didn't depend on our circumstances. God was still here, regardless.

When the service ended, Mac slipped out to get Gabe from the children's building. Maybe Les would still be around after he picked up his son. But his friend was nowhere in sight when Mac returned to the foyer. His aunt and Harry stood by the worship center doors with Miss Connie and Rachel.

"There you are. We've all decided to go the Morning Glory for lunch." Aunt Sharon's brown eyes looked to have an extra shine as she stood beside Harry.

Good for her. Good for Harry. They'd known each since they were kids. But Aunt Sharon's announcement was as welcome as hearing that cattle prices had plummeted. He didn't want to be anywhere near Rachel Landry—or any other woman his aunt wanted to fix him up with.

Gabe's face lit up. "Can I have chicken strips?"

Mac didn't have the heart to disappoint his son. "Sure thing."

Too soon, he parked his truck in the lot behind the Morning Glory Café. His aunt had ridden with Harry. Maybe that's why she'd been trying to push him to look for a girlfriend, in spite of how often he said he wasn't interested. He might as well have told his horse. Boots would have listened better.

"Table for six, Misty." Miss Connie made her announcement to the hostess the second everyone entered.

The happy tone of the elderly lady's voice wasn't Mac's imagination. His aunt and Harry looked just as cheerful. Rachel's thin smile appeared too stiff to be real. That improved his opinion of her. Fighting off matchmakers might be the only thing they had in common.

When their table was ready, Harry, Aunt Sharon and Miss Connie left three empty chairs next to each other at the round table. Mac seated Gabe in the middle one. He chose the spot to his son's left. Rachel took the chair to Gabe's right. One small way to thwart the well-meaning trio paying too close attention to him and Rachel.

Gabe grabbed the little package of crayons sitting on his children's menu. "Open these, Daddy?"

"What do you say?"

"Please."

Mac handed the crayons to his son. With only one café in town, he knew everything they offered here without looking. So did the others.

Rachel kept her head down as she studied her menu. Only a chef would read every word the way she looked to be doing. Or someone just as irritated with the current situation as Mac was. How he hoped the latter was true.

"Want to play tic-tac-toe, Daddy?" Gabe slid his menu closer to Mac.

"Yeah."

Mac picked up a crayon. Let everyone else talk about the weather or the latest happenings in Sunrise. Rachel didn't look up from her menu. She'd had time to read it more than once. The current situation must not make her any happier than it did him.

By the time their food came, the three conspirators had mentioned the upcoming fund-raiser for the library and the score of Friday night's football game, plus how hot it was today for September. Mac and Rachel chimed in here and there while he and Gabe colored.

"Are you having fun in kindergarten?" Rachel turned to Gabe while Mac cut up the chicken strips for his son.

"I don't go yet."

"He turned five after Labor Day, so next year." Mac grinned at his son.

Gabe nodded. "Uh-huh. Next year."

Rachel soon knew about Gabe's recent birthday party and every toy he'd been given. If she didn't like kids, she was an excellent actress. The way she gave Gabe her full attention as he talked signaled her interest might be genuine. But she'd be gone in a few weeks. Unlike his ex, at least she was honest about not staying in town.

Lance Gardner walked over to their table. "How is everyone doing?"

"We're all fine. The food's great as usual, Lance." Harry stabbed a bite of his pork chop with his fork.

"That's what I like to hear." Lance's smile looked to be aimed more at Rachel than anyone else. "Rachel, thanks for coming back. We don't get a Dallas chef here often."

She set her tea glass next to her plate. "You've got a nice place."

"You're welcome to come by and talk shop anytime."

"Thanks, but right now I'm focusing on helping Granna."

"Whenever you can would be great."

Rachel shrugged. "We'll see."

Lance nodded and walked off to talk to other guests.

To keep anyone from guessing how pleased he was that Rachel acted so unimpressed with Lance, Mac looked down to butter another roll. He was much happier than he should be to see the man walk away so soon. He had to not let this woman get to him. His reaction was too much. Why she snagged his attention at all made no sense at all. But she'd practically done the same thing on Friday.

As they ate, Rachel kept talking to Gabe and asking him questions. Mac supplied explanations when needed. By the time they'd finished eating, they had had a better conversation than he'd intended.

"Miss Rachel, will you sit by me if we come back another time?" Gabe skipped beside her when they all headed to their vehicles.

Since Mac had to keep hold of Gabe's hand, he had no choice but to walk with Rachel, too. The other three kept their distance, keeping several steps ahead of them. He really needed to figure out how to convince them that their obvious matchmaking wouldn't work.

"I'd be happy to sit by you again."

Gabe's face shone. "Me, too." He reached for Rachel's hand with his free one. "Walk with me and Daddy to our truck?"

She glanced over to her grandmother, still talking to Aunt Sharon and Harry. "Looks like I've got time for that."

Mac would be finding excuses to head straight home after church for however long Rachel stayed here. As uninterested as she'd been acting, she might do the same. But her instant willingness to talk about a next time to sit by Gabe spooked him. So did the fact his son still held her hand. He couldn't let his son get attached to a Dallas woman who would soon be gone.

They walked in silence the rest of the way to Mac's truck. Rachel looked toward her grandmother again while he made sure Gabe was buckled into his car seat.

"Um, in case you don't know, my grandmother is an unapologetic matchmaker." She kept her voice low.

Straightening to look at her, he swallowed the sarcastic words that came to mind. Everyone around here knew about Miss Connie's love for meddling. She'd tried more than once to "help" him with his love life.

Rachel took a deep breath. "Please don't take this the wrong way, but I don't want to date you—or anyone—right now."

With a comment like that, the perceptive woman had all but roped the moon. "Agreed. Friendship is all I want, no matter what my aunt might be hinting. We won't be in church next Sunday, so you'll get a rest."

"Good—I mean, okay." She laughed. "Then again, I don't want to be the reason why you're avoiding church."

He chuckled. "Not at all. We have a small bed-and-breakfast set up at our ranch. Aunt Sharon and I take turns on Sunday with the couple who handles the weekend guests for us, so they can come to church, too."

"How nice."

"Oh, Mac." Aunt Sharon waved at him from a few cars over. "Harry will bring me home later."

After such an honest conversation with Rachel, the grin he tossed his aunt's direction was genuine. "If we're lucky, they'll start concentrating on each other so much that they'll leave us alone."

She looked toward Miss Connie's car. "I'd better get Granna home."

"'Bye, Miss Rachel." Gabe waved at her.

"'Bye, Gabe. Have fun with your dog this afternoon." She paused to wave back.

Mac glanced over her shoulder to see all three conspirators looking as if they'd won the lottery. He and Rachel would have to be careful or the whole town would have them paired off, thanks to the well-meaning trio smiling their way.

He'd made a colossal mistake talking to Rachel Landry alone.

Chapter Two

Rachel shut the door to the wood cabinet under the countertop microwave. By ten o'clock Thursday morning, she'd reorganized every shelf to make it easier for Granna to reach the things she used the most—another chore Granna's arthritis made it almost impossible for her to do. Hopefully it was another way to show her she needed to hire someone to help her. Next week, she'd tackle the closets. Then what?

"Everything looks so nice. Thank you, sugar." Granna kissed Rachel's cheek.

"You're welcome. I think I'll go for a walk, since it's cooler. And I need to return my library book." She had plenty of time before she needed to set things out for lunch. "Want to come?"

"Not today. You need time to yourself."

"I could never get tired of you." Which was true, but she was craving time alone after so much people time lately at church.

"I'll come with you another day." Granna patted Rachel's cheek.

Rachel went to get her clutch and phone from her room. She probably wouldn't need either one, but old habits were hard to break. So was not grabbing her pepper spray. You could take the girl out of the city, but not the city out of the girl.

She breathed in the fall air as she stepped outside. No use wasting a seventy-degree morning when the highs could still be over ninety this time of year.

Granna's next-door neighbors had set out yellow and purple pansies in their front flowerbed. Maybe she should spruce up Granna's yard. But her grandmother didn't want or need the extra work caring for plants. Since she had a yardman, Granna must realize that.

Still, Granna could do a lot more than Dad and Aunt Michelle had told Rachel she could do. All her grandmother really needed was help with housekeeping and someone to fix meals for her and to take her places out of town, where she shouldn't be driving.

A neighbor waved as Rachel reached the end of the street. She waved back. In Dallas, she'd barely known anyone in her entire apartment complex. Life in a small town like Sunrise was different, in a good way.

Others nodded and smiled at her as she walked into the main area of town. The flower-filled urns on each corner made her walk more picturesque than going through her old neighborhood She strolled toward the library on the next street. Reading a book in a matter of days hadn't happened since before she'd attended culinary school. Her two days off had so often been reduced to Monday only that she'd gotten used to barely having time to think.

She was determined that her next job would have better hours. And dating or falling in love with her boss wouldn't happen again.

If she could only figure out what her next job would be…

"Hi, Rachel." Straw hat in hand, Mac stepped out of the library as she walked up the steps.

Of all the days she could have picked to return her book. "Hi." How often did this man come to town? Didn't he have to be with his cows or something?

He grinned. "I had an advisory board meeting they said we couldn't handle online. You look as surprised to see me as I am to see you."

She'd never been good at keeping her emotions off her face.

His brown eyes twinkled. "We've got to stop meeting like this."

Her laugh slipped out on its own. "We do. I won't tell Granna if you won't tell your aunt."

"Deal." Mac raised his hand in a mock pledge.

"I promise this won't happen again. I would have resigned today, but next month's fund-raiser was my idea. So I'll see that through, then quit since they want more in-person than online meetings." His grin widened.

"That sounds good. I mean, good for you." Good for her, too, if they saw less of each other. This friendly, honest man was too easy to like. Too easy to look at with his broad shoulders and expressive, smiling eyes.

"Yeah, it's good."

What a strange conversation. They both sounded so callous. But she meant every word she said. She hoped he did.

His expression sobered. "So you know, next month's fund-raiser is an old-fashioned box supper. Men bid on the women's baskets, and the ladies eat with the winning bidders. Some of the single guys might be looking forward to the whole thing."

She shuddered. "I doubt I'll be here next month."

"Yeah, but after what my aunt and your grandmother seem to be planning, I thought I'd better give you a heads-up."

"Thanks for the warning, but I'm sure I'll be back in Dallas by then." She was sure she wouldn't be around to share a meal with this man.

"I understand. If I couldn't bid on my aunt's basket, I'd find an excuse to stay home."

"What if Harry wants her basket?"

"I hadn't thought of that." He tapped his chin. "Pray for rain. Or I guess I could bid on Miss Connie's basket if the weather's better than I'd like."

"Granna's a good cook, but I'll be happy to pray for rain, too." Why a good-looking rancher only wanted to bid on older ladies' baskets seemed strange. She supposed it was none of her business.

He checked his watch. "I've got work to do, so instead of being polite and mansplaining ranching or something to you, I'll be rude and walk away."

"I'm sure I'll get over it." His sense of humor and sarcasm made running into him a pleasant accident. Someone listening to them might shake their heads at such sarcasm. But she understood completely where he was coming from, so a little humor was fine. And his warning about the box supper raised her opinion of him considerably. But she wouldn't tell him. Especially because it was too hard to look away from his tanned face and warm smile.

He nodded before heading to his truck parked a few feet away. Half an hour later, she carried out the second library book she'd checked out in years. Might as well enjoy this downtime while she could. She probably didn't have too long until her grandmother decided she was taking advantage of Rachel and insisted on hiring someone to help her. Dad and Aunt Michelle's plan would work to perfection when that happened.

But then Rachel would have to figure out a plan for herself. Facing reality again wouldn't be as rewarding as this special time with Granna.

Leaving the little downtown area, she walked past the playground, where a couple of mothers watched their preschoolers play. The scene reminded her of home. She missed seeing her niece and nephews.

There was a path around the small pond nearby, but there was no one around. Maybe she'd found somewhere in this little town she could finally be alone. But not for too long. She didn't want her grandmother worrying about how much Rachel liked and wanted solitude. Alone meant being safe, where no man could hurt her again—something her matchmaking grandmother didn't understand at all.

Granna's expression brightened as soon as she saw Rachel step into the living room, where the TV blared a little louder than Rachel liked. "Did you have a nice walk?"

"I did. I checked out another book." A mystery novel with no mention of romance on the back cover.

"Good. I thought of something I'd like help with after lunch."

"That's what I'm here for." Rachel set her book on the end table by the couch. "Should we have leftover chicken noodle soup for lunch?"

"I'll eat your homemade soup any time. Then you can help me organize family pictures."

"That will be fun."

They spent an enjoyable afternoon sitting next to each other looking through boxes and albums of pictures. Granna had photos going back to her grandparents. Rachel soaked in every story her grandmother wanted to tell.

"You should write all this down so everyone knows who these people are and what they did. I can't begin to remember everything you've told me, no matter how hard I try." Rachel set a postcard written to her great-grandmother on the coffee table in front of them.

"That might be my next project." Granna glowed. She grabbed the TV remote to turn on the early news.

Rachel's heart felt as warm as her grandmother's happy smile. She was so happy to have this precious time with Granna. But she was starting to worry about going home. Where was home anymore?

Her mother's words about finding a new home and not losing who she was ran unbidden through her mind. It had been one of the last things Mom had told her before she got in her car to drive to Sunrise. After reminding her how at home Rachel had felt in the little bistro she'd worked in right out of culinary school.

Maybe leaving such a welcoming place hadn't been right after all. Another mistake she didn't want to think about.

"I'll go read awhile before it's time to start dinner." Losing herself in a book was better than thinking about things that still hurt too much to remember.

When Rachel was halfway through the third chapter, Granna's phone rang. Granna answered on the second ring, so Rachel went back to her book.

The grandmother clock in the living room chimed five times. Granna was still talking on the phone to someone. She sounded happy. Rachel set her book on the nightstand next to her bed. Not *her* bed. Every piece of furniture she owned was in storage in Dallas. But Granna's house had been home since before she could remember. One place she'd always belonged.

Granna set her cordless phone on the coffee table as Rachel came into the living room. "I had a great talk with Sharon Greer. She invited us to supper on Saturday at their ranch."

"She did?"

"Yes. Mac is grilling burgers. I told her we'd be happy to bring vegetables or salad and dessert." Her ear-to-ear grin reminded Rachel of a child who'd just gotten everything she'd asked for at Christmas. "Really, I assumed since you love to cook, you wouldn't mind fixing all that."

"Of course not." She hoped her face didn't give away her true thoughts. Granna meant well.

She still enjoyed cooking. For family. Maybe not professionally anymore. Definitely not for a man Granna thought she should be dating. Granna wouldn't want to hear that Rachel would rather go to a rattlesnake roundup than eat supper with Mac Greer at his house.

Granna and Sharon would have planned something even if Rachel had stayed. She'd been prepared to dodge Granna's matching efforts, never realizing Sharon Greer would be a willing partner. They were definitely trying to push her and Mac together. At least Mac would be happy to help Rachel thwart both women.

Chapter Three

"Are you gonna fix a little burger just for me?" Gabe asked as he stood at Mac's side in the kitchen. He'd been a watchful helper since he was big enough to stand on the little yellow stool he now occupied.

"Just for you, the way I always do." Mac sprinkled seasoning mix on the platter full of meat patties. "This little one is yours."

Their ritual comforted him. But not completely. Rachel and Miss Connie should be here around five o'clock. Since burgers cooked quickly, he'd wait to put them on the grill outside until their guests came. It would be a good way to avoid Rachel for a little while.

The doorbell rang. The dog barked.

"They're here!" Gabe hopped to the floor, then rushed toward the front door.

In no hurry to leave the kitchen, Mac took his time washing and drying his hands. But he couldn't be rude and not greet their guests. He placed one boot in front of the other as he trudged to the living room.

"We're so glad y'all came." Aunt Sharon ushered in Miss Connie, followed by Rachel not far behind.

"Thank y'all for inviting us." Miss Connie's smile broadened as Mac walked into the room.

"Where do you want these baked beans?" Rachel held out a dish that smelled so good his stomach growled.

"I'll take that to the kitchen." Aunt Sharon reached for the food.

"There's plenty more in the car." Miss Connie seated herself in the chair closest to the couch. The dog walked over to her for a pat on his head. The silver-haired lady obliged him. "Rachel cooked enough for half of Sunrise."

"I'll help carry things in." Mac's good manners wouldn't allow him to not help Rachel. His common sense had hoped for a way to avoid being alone with her.

He matched Rachel's shorter stride to follow her to Miss Connie's Camry.

"You know that Granna and your aunt cooked this up on the phone the other night, right?" Rachel said as she grabbed the handle for the back door.

"Believe me. I heard. I'll take whatever's the heaviest."

"Nothing's hard to carry. But I'll take the blue plastic cake container. If my chocolate torte layers slide before I finish putting them together, I can't be mad at anyone but me."

"Sounds good." He had no idea what a torte was. But anything chocolate would make Gabe happy. Him, too.

She grabbed a small soft cooler from the floor to

hand to Mac. "I made potato salad in case someone doesn't like the fresh broccoli dish."

"Good idea. Gabe thinks someone is torturing him if they set one bite of broccoli on his plate."

Since Mac could carry the cooler with one hand, he closed the car doors for her. She carried the cake plate with both hands, keeping it level. Carefully, she stepped toward the house.

He set the cooler on the countertop closest to the refrigerator. Then grabbed the platter full of hamburger patties. "I'll put these on the grill."

No one bothered him as he kept watch over the meat. His aunt probably would have planned something different if she'd realized burgers would be a good way for him to spend a little less time with Rachel. Too bad he didn't have a cow calving that he needed to check on.

By the time Mac carried the fully cooked hamburgers inside, Harry was standing in the kitchen with the women, as close to Aunt Sharon as he could get without being in the way. He never took his eyes off her as she sliced a tomato.

"Those burgers smell delicious." Harry glanced up at Mac.

Mac grinned as he covered them with foil. Strange how he'd never thought about his fifty-five-year-old unmarried aunt having a boyfriend. The woman had taught English and other classes in exotic places all over the world. Dad would be in for a shock when he came home and saw his little sister so interested in Harry.

"I think we've got everything set out. We can eat

as soon as we pray." Aunt Sharon stepped away from the counter.

While still standing, she held one hand out to Harry, the other to Gabe. Harry took Miss Connie's hand as they formed a circle. Leaving him no choice but to take Gabe's hand to his left and Rachel's to his right. Her soft hand fit his too well.

Everyone looked to him to say grace. He bowed his head. He hoped God didn't mind hearing the shortest prayer Mac could remember saying in a long time. That God didn't mind how holding Rachel's hand rattled him so much he had a hard time concentrating on being thankful for the food they were about to eat.

The second he said, "Amen," Rachel slipped her fingers from his.

"Now we can eat." Gabe grabbed a yellow paper plate from the top of the stack on the countertop.

A black plate would have better matched Mac's mood. "Let me help you." He busied himself filling Gabe's plate and helping him put his burger together.

He fixed his own plate last. Aunt Sharon had Gabe sit at one end of the table and Harry next to her. Miss Connie took the other end chair, leaving the only empty spot next to Rachel. Playing the considerate host had cost him. Good manners were more like a curse lately. With nothing good about them. Especially since he kept finding more things to like about Rachel.

Everyone praised the side dishes she had made. Gabe even took a taste of the broccoli salad. Or whatever it was called. It looked something like a salad with bacon pieces and onions tossed in.

"Can we have dessert now?" Gabe licked his lips after he finished the last bite of his baked beans. "Miss Rachel let me lick the bowls after she put the icing on the cake. She stacked everything up pretty."

He doubted a chef would have used the word *stacked* to describe her dessert. But the smile she gave Gabe added one more reason to like her.

No. He wouldn't go there. Memories of the way Alicia had deserted him and their almost two-year-old son still hurt.

"I'll bring it out if everyone's ready for dessert." Rachel scooted her chair back.

The woman dressed in a gold shirt and loose-fitting khaki-colored pants was a welcome interruption to his morose thoughts. She looked much better than his current mood.

"I'll get the dessert plates." Aunt Sharon headed to the kitchen.

Rachel soon returned carrying a four-layer chocolate cake. It looked liked a delicious, gooey mess. No wonder she'd waited to put it together here and let Gabe lick bowls.

"I took a picture of this to send to Caroline." Aunt Sharon followed Rachel back into the room. "She'd love this."

His aunt was right. Mom would thoroughly enjoy such a fancy-looking dessert. She'd get along great with Rachel. No. He wouldn't go there. That was a dangerous path to travel. He refocused his attention on the cake Rachel was slicing.

His mouth started to water.

When he took his first bite, he wasn't disappointed. "Very good."

Rachel smiled and said, "Thank you."

"When we drove up to the gate, Rachel asked me how your ranch got the name Still Waters. I told her to let a Greer tell her that story." Miss Connie grinned in Mac's direction.

"Mac tells it best." His aunt looked straight across to him.

The moist bite of cake he'd just popped into his mouth turned drier than dust and just as hard to swallow. The two matchmaking friends were up to something. Again.

"You're the one named after your granddad. So you should give Rachel a short tour of the ranch while you tell her why he picked that name." His footwear-loving aunt looked as happy as if she'd just brought home half the store on sale.

"Sure, I could do that." He looked over at Rachel, hoping she'd quickly think of a way to dodge the trap laid for them.

"I can't leave you to clean up everything." She looked down as she wiped her mouth with her napkin.

"I'll help with that." Harry looked happy to do his share to spring the trap.

"I'm not helpless." Miss Connie looked in his and Rachel's direction as well. "The two of you fixed all this good food. We'll clean up."

"And Gabe can help. You're a good helper. Aren't you, Gabe?"

Aunt Sharon knew Gabe loved to help her any time.

The woman was shameless when it came to match-making lately. So shameless she'd take advantage of a five-year-old. His son's enthusiastic nod made Mac wonder if Gabe had been coached ahead of Not the way he'd planned to finish the rest of his dessert. Or his evening. Getting by with small talk would have been rough enough.

As she settled into the passenger seat of Mac's truck, Rachel felt slightly awkward. She'd never been alone with Mac in such an enclosed space. She wasn't sure how she felt about that. But before she had time to worry, Mac said, "They did it again." He shook his head as he put the key into the ignition of his truck.

"They sure did."

She waited for his usual humor or teasing. But he drove without saying a word. She looked out the window at the gently rolling land of the ranch.

The sun burned just above the horizon as they approached a fence. A few black cows stood not far away. The peaceful view was the opposite of the turmoil she'd experienced too much of lately. Nothing had been peaceful in Dallas for too long, and she'd missed all the hints that things might be other than ideal about her job or her love life.

Enough of that. She'd wasn't here of her own choice, but no use spoiling this beautiful view.

"I did wonder why your ranch is called Still Waters. But I had no idea everyone would use that to send us off on a drive so you could answer a simple question."

She broke the uncomfortable silence hanging between them. Judging from his stiff posture, he wasn't any happier than she was with their current situation.

"It's a story I don't mind telling." He loosened his grip on the steering wheel.

She waited, hoping he'd soon let her know the tale of the Still Waters ranch. Instead he looked straight ahead again.

"So the only cows you've ever seen are from a road?"

She nodded. His kind expression set her at ease. A little. He wasn't making fun of her for not knowing anything about his way of life. She did like that.

He stopped the truck. "Want to get out and walk up to the fence?"

"Okay."

In case he planned to walk around and open her door, she hopped out of the truck as quickly as possible. He walked next to her, but not too close.

"I'll let you look a minute or two so you can tell everyone you've seen cows up close while they're grazing in a pasture. Then we'll head to the creek so I can tell my family story right." He leaned against the wooden fence post.

She tried to pretend an interest in the animals a short distance away. Tried to pretend she'd rather not focus on the considerate man beside her. The guy who didn't question why she only wanted his friendship. Who didn't push her for more. She'd never seen him at ease the way he was now. He belonged here. On this land, this ranch.

How she longed to find a place like this for herself. A place she could belong. Somewhere to be at peace again.

"We raise Black Angus," he said, glancing her way.

"Good-quality beef." She hoped her words didn't sound too inane, since beef was not what she was concerned about just now.

"Yeah. It is." He grinned. "It looks a little different on the hoof, I imagine."

"It does." She tried to sound more enthusiastic than she felt. But she hadn't planned on staring at walking prime rib today.

"Let's go to the creek before the sun sets." He straightened.

She followed him back to the truck. Silence descended between them again. She had no idea what to say to him. Friendship with such a nice guy shouldn't be this awkward, should it? Maybe it wouldn't be if Granna and her friends weren't trying so hard to match her and Mac together.

The tranquil scene outside her window reminded her of a landscape painting dotted with black cows eating grass. No—grazing in a pasture. That's what Mac had called it.

"Here's our own piece of Longhorn Creek before it eventually ends up in the Colorado River." Mac stopped the truck close to a path leading down to what must be the creek he'd mentioned.

"Longhorn Creek?"

The mischievous twinkle she'd wanted to see finally sparked in his eyes. "This area's had ranches since the late 1800s. Somebody got real creative with the name."

She couldn't help but return his grin. "So this creek helps you tell your ranch story?"

"Yeah."

He led her down the narrow path that ended in what looked like a miniature park. The babbling creek might lull someone to sleep if they sat too long on any of the three inviting-looking wooden benches near the water's edge. Trees and the other vegetation had been trimmed away to keep from blocking the view, which stretched all the way to the horizon, where the soon-to-be-setting sun was turning into wondrous shades of lavender, pink and yellow.

"This is so beautiful."

"Our family's private piece of peace."

"I see what you mean." She closed her eyes and breathed in the fresh air. Breathed in the peace she so desperately needed.

"Want to hear Granddad's story?"

He spoke so quietly she couldn't help wondering if this place affected him the way it did her.

"I'd like that." She'd like to know any story connected to this tranquil spot.

"Any of these three brown wooden benches are comfortable and a great place for storytelling. We fixed a little mini park for the ranch guests so they can sit on the river bank and soak in the peace while they're here." He gestured toward them.

She sat on one end. He took the other, leaving enough space between them for another person if someone else was here. He kept his gaze focused straight ahead.

"Granddaddy was a tail gunner in the Army Air Corps during World War II. He died almost five years ago. We were close…"

Not sure why he let his sentence go unfinished, Rachel waited until he decided to continue. Granna hadn't hinted the Greer story was an unhappy one. Maybe talking about his beloved grandfather could still be hard for Mac.

"Like most true heroes, he never told us much about the war. We know one plane he was in got shot down over the ocean. After he bailed out, dolphins pushed him to shore."

She remained silent, because saying too much didn't fit in such a quiet place, where the comfortable silence was broken only by singing birds and clear water running over rocks.

"He came home after the war to help his parents run their farm in Alabama. But they were killed along with his only sister in a car accident about six months later."

"How awful."

Mac nodded. "So Granddaddy sold the farm. His best buddy in the air corps was a Texan who said this would be a good place to start over. My grandfather fell in love with this area and his buddy's sister, my grandmother. They bought this ranch not long after they married."

He paused again. She waited for him to continue.

"Granddaddy said they picked the name Still Waters the first time he and Meemaw walked to this creek. They felt as if God had led them to their own green pastures and still waters. To their home. Just like the still waters in Psalm 23."

Rachel had no words. The Greers had built a loving home in this place. A lasting home for their generations.

A Dallas restaurant the last two years. What a contrast between the Greers's legacy and her own lack of insight.

The deep longing for her own home with still waters overwhelmed her as she listened to the soothing sounds of the creek running a couple of feet in front of her. The creek had a home to go to as it made its way to the Colorado River.

Where was her home?

Chapter Four

Mac stared at the computer screen in front of him, trying to concentrate on his accounting. Finishing up chores a couple of hours before supper hardly ever happened. He could enter his latest expenses during daylight hours for a change instead of waiting until after Gabe had gone to bed. But thoughts of Rachel made it hard to think about numbers.

She had soaked in every word of his story about the ranch's name, listening more carefully than anyone else he could remember. Then they'd sat quietly, staring off at the sunset, as if the view he never got tired of intrigued her as much as it did him. Alicia had hated sitting still.

Rachel respected his need for distance, no questions asked. No scooting closer to him as they sat on the same bench. No flirting. They'd watched the sun go down. She'd gasped in awe at such a beautiful sight. Neither of them had said much.

If she wasn't going back to the big city soon, they

might become genuine friends. He'd never felt so comfortable sitting in silence with someone. Or so scared, since he hadn't been able to get the woman off his mind since Saturday.

Three days ago. He dared not let himself become more comfortable with her, no matter how easy she was to be with. Liking her was dangerous enough. Moving beyond that was too risky to consider. She'd head back to Dallas the minute Miss Connie didn't need help anymore.

He forced his attention back to the accounting program in front of him. He'd been in his office a good twenty minutes and had only entered this month's electric bill. *Focus*. He typed in what he'd spent on new fence posts and barbed wire last week.

Thirty minutes later, he'd caught up on all the book work. He clicked over to check the updated totals for the year. After he'd had to hire a temporary cook and wrangler to replace his mom and dad, the guest ranch was barely breaking even. Good thing beef prices were holding steady right now. His parents would be expecting Mac's usual Tuesday night call. Too bad he couldn't give them better news.

Catching his parents up by phone still felt strange. The only time they hadn't worked together was the couple of years he'd gone off to college, when he'd thought Dad should modernize the way he did things.

But all college had taught him was how much he hated being away from the ranch. How much he hated big cities. Fort Worth was as far east as he cared to go.

Living in an overcrowded, noisy place like Dallas was his idea of a nightmare.

A light tap on the door frame interrupted his thoughts.

"Mac, can we talk to you?" The cook, Lisa, and her husband, Dan stood in the hall.

"Sure. Come in." Mac rose.

Both of them looked as if they were watching their steps to keep from tripping over their own feet. It was so unlike them, as they usually looked everyone directly in the eye. Something wasn't right.

Dan sucked in a breath. "We got a call from our daughter. Out in Mesquite. Her doctor put her on bed rest so the baby won't come too soon."

"I'm sorry. I'll pray for her." Judging from Dan's distraught tone, Mac had the feeling the bad news was just getting started.

"We know you will, but…" Dan and his wife exchanged worried looks. "She needs help with her two boys. Since her husband has to work, Lisa and I are the only ones who can come stay with her."

"Okay…" Mac suspected he wasn't going to like whatever else Dan was struggling to say.

"So we're going to have to leave as soon as we can pack up our things." Lisa's words rushed out as she clasped and unclasped her hands in front of her. "We hate to do this with no notice, and—"

"It's all right. Your daughter and grandchild are more important than the guests coming here later this week."

The worry lines on Lisa's face relaxed a little. "Thanks, Mac. We're so sorry to do this to you."

Mac shook his head. "Don't worry about me. Go

pack. I'll have your checks ready so you can take them with you when you leave."

"Thanks." Dan extended his hand. "We appreciate all your family has done for us."

"You're welcome." Mac was amazed how relaxed he sounded as he shook hands with the man.

Calmly standing in the middle of a whirlwind pretending everything around him wasn't blowing in more directions than he could count. He sank into his desk chair as soon as the Thompsons left the room. *Now what?*

Mac had no idea how to replace them both in the next three days.

After he finished cutting their paychecks, he went to find Aunt Sharon. She'd become his go-to person for someone to talk to since his parents couldn't be here. He hoped she was still weeding flowerbeds and hadn't gone exploring somewhere with Gabe. Crazy relief flooded through him as he spied her kneeling at the edge of the flowers in the front yard. For once, she'd stayed where she'd said she'd be. Plus, Gabe and his dog played not too far away.

"Looks like you finished your paperwork." She pulled on a weed as he walked up to her.

"Yes, ma'am. We need to talk. Could we go in the house where it's cooler, please?"

"Oh?" She pushed a strand of black hair out of her face as she looked up at him. "Something wrong?"

He nodded. "Gabe, come play closer to the house. Aunt Sharon and I are heading inside."

"We'll have to talk in the kitchen unless you want

to give me time to change and clean up first. I won't sit on the couch in these dirty clothes."

"The kitchen's fine."

The short walk to the back of the house gave Mac the time he needed to tell his aunt about their unexpected problems.

"We'll make it through this, too." She slipped off her dirt-caked tennis shoes before walking inside.

"Yes, ma'am, but I haven't thought of just how yet."

She grabbed a pitcher of sweet tea from the refrigerator. "Want some?"

"Please." Mac took his usual spot at the table. His rightfully thirsty aunt would take her time. Pushing her to hurry with anything made her even slower.

"No need to worry about finding a cook so quickly. We not only know a cook who's out of work, we know a *chef*." She grinned as she set a glass in front of him.

He shook his head. "Miss Connie needs Rachel's help more than we need a cook."

"No. Connie's got something in the works for help but says she can't say what it is right now. When Rachel needed to come here awhile to think and decide about her next job, Connie wasn't about to tell her no." She sipped her tea. "So Connie will be okay. And you'll be fine hiring Rachel."

No, he wouldn't. He had enough trouble ignoring her every other Sunday. He didn't need her here on the ranch a few days a week cooking. But he had no other choice.

She emptied her glass, then set it on the table. "Which means we hire Rachel. Connie says Rachel seems lost without a job but still doesn't know what she wants to do." Her wide grin returned. "So we'll help Rachel while she helps us."

"If she agrees to work for us."

"I'm confident that a woman as sweet as she is will be happy to help us out of such a tight jam."

No use arguing with his aunt over something she'd already decided would happen. Rachel might need to find her way again. But he didn't need to lose his way by caring too much for her or any other woman.

"I'll call Connie and see if Rachel will be home after supper."

Her sparkling eyes meant she'd talk about a lot more than a job offer. Too bad his aunt and Miss Connie had hit it off so well lately.

He shook his head. "I'll call, since I'm the one who's hoping to hire her." *Hoping* was not the right word. *Needed* to hire her, yes. Hoped, no. He'd ask anybody else first if he knew anybody else. But he didn't. So he'd offer the job to Rachel.

A temporary job. His parents should be home in about six weeks. For the sake of the ranch, he could handle seeing Rachel that long on a regular basis.

He parked his truck in Miss Connie's driveway a few minutes after seven o'clock. After taking several deep breaths, he climbed out. Before he had a chance to knock on the front door, he heard Miss Connie telling Rachel he was here. Which meant the curtain he'd seen moving in the front window must have been from an elderly lady watching for him.

Only six more weeks until his parents came home.

Six weeks of fending off the matchmaking. Something told him Miss Connie and Aunt Sharon might make it feel more like six years.

Rachel ushered Mac into the living room. "You said you need to ask me a favor?"

He nodded. "I know my call didn't make much sense, but I wanted to talk to you in person."

"Okay…" She couldn't imagine what this was all about. But Granna's imagination was working overtime, so Rachel would wait to hear what Mac wanted rather than guess.

"Hello, Mac." Granna rose from her spot on the couch. "Would you like some tea, maybe some cookies? Rachel made my favorite chocolate chip ones."

"No, thanks, Miss Connie."

"Then I'll go watch TV in my room." Granna grabbed her cane. "Rachel, you tell him yes."

"About what?"

"About helping him out. Sharon texted me a little while ago. I won't hear you saying no." She tossed them a grin over her shoulder as she left the room.

Rachel seated herself on the beige couch. Mac took the antique side chair angled a couple of feet away. His jeans and chambray shirt made him look so out of place sitting on the rose-pink cushioned chair. His stiff posture didn't help matters.

"Our cook and wrangler left this afternoon with no notice. They have to go help their daughter, who's having complications with her pregnancy." He paused as he sucked in a deep breath. "So I came to ask if you could help me out until my parents come home."

"Help you out how?"

"Come cook for our ranch guests. We have anywhere from two to six people staying on the ranch most weekends and some during the week once in a while."

"I don't know…" What he was describing would be a part-time job compared to the hours she'd worked in Dallas. It sounded like an easy, stress-free job. Which made his offer tempting. Except she'd be working closely with him. Saying yes should be out of the question.

"I'm flattered you thought of me." Which she was, but this didn't fit in with her plan to help Granna at all. "But can't you find someone around here who's more used to working on a ranch?"

"Probably not. Our reputation as a guest ranch has as much to do with the food as the trail rides and Western atmosphere we offer."

"I see." Except she didn't. Couldn't envision herself ever working on any ranch.

"I'd ask somebody else if I knew someone who could do what we need."

He looked miserable. Which made her feel even worse. The poor man was dealing with an unplanned emergency already.

"It wouldn't be for long."

"You said part-time, mostly weekends?" She wasn't sure she wanted the job. But the idea of cooking again appealed to her more than she'd thought it would.

"You could stay with your grandmother on the days

we don't need you. Aunt Sharon and I will work out taking your place every other Sunday for lunch so you can make it to church some weeks."

"That sounds good."

This might be a doable way to ease herself out of Granna's life while testing to see if she wanted to cook professionally again.

"What might work out best is if you stayed at the ranch from Thursday afternoon till Sunday after lunch. Except for this week, you should come on Wednesday, because our cook, Lisa, left so many things undone."

"It only takes me about thirty minutes to get out there for dinner, so I might make the drive every day." She'd stay in Sunrise if at all possible. Except tomorrow was Wednesday. She needed more time to think than that.

"Mom would get up by five on Saturdays and Sundays to have breakfast ready at eight."

"Oh. In that case, staying there weekends would make sense." Then she asked, "Why do you think I'd have to be there Thursday nights, too?"

"Thursday afternoon is the best day to buy groceries, since we usually know by then how many guests we'll have for the weekend. Sometimes we even know by late Wednesday. If you didn't stay on Thursday, you'd have to be up early Friday to drive out and put groceries away. Mom or Lisa spent most of Friday getting ready for the weekend."

"I see." He hadn't said how involved he'd be with the guests. But he wouldn't be cooking, so she should be fine if she took the job.

He shifted. The ill-fitted chair probably wasn't the

only thing making him uncomfortable. He didn't look or sound the least bit happy to be offering her this job.

"You'd have your own place to stay, upstairs over the guest dining room and commercial kitchen. It includes two bedrooms, a small kitchen, a sitting area and a bathroom."

Her eyes widened. All that space sounded larger than her Dallas apartment had been the last few years. Another lure for a job she shouldn't be thinking of taking. "I'm not sure Granna can do without my help that long at a time. And…"

Granna didn't need near as much help as her dad and aunt had said. But this was not the way she wanted the Lord to show her how to ease herself out of her grandmother's life. Out of Sunrise. Back to a place with shopping, movies and specialty grocery stores. Working at Mac's ranch would make it even easier for Granna and Sharon to try to pair her off with Mac. That was not the kind of escape she wanted or needed.

"Aunt Sharon says there are ladies who would be happy to come help Miss Connie. Everybody around here loves her."

"That's probably what they were texting about behind our backs." Rachel didn't want to imagine how happy both women were about Mac needing her help. How she wished her dad hadn't showed Granna how to text.

"Probably. We'd need you to work for about four weeks. Six weeks, max. I'd ask someone else if I could, but we have guests coming in Friday." He leaned toward her, tapping his hat on his leg. "I wasn't kidding when I said I needed a huge favor."

"No, you weren't."

His obvious desperation was palpable. So was the tug on her heart as soon as he'd mentioned her cooking for his guests. Maybe this temporary job would be a good way to see if she wanted to cook again or try a different career.

"If I can work something out for Granna, I might be able to help you. Tell me more about being a chef at a guest ranch."

As if someone had cut the straps to the board at his back, his entire body relaxed. "Most guests arrive on Friday afternoon or early evening. So they'd need supper on Friday night. Breakfast on Saturday. We generally offer a light lunch on Saturday, because I smoke brisket and ribs for a ranch-type supper on Saturday night. And then on Sunday we have a fancy brunch. Checkout is around 1:00 p.m."

"What kind of breakfast do you prefer be served? What do you consider a light lunch? Sandwiches? What's fancy to you?"

He grinned. "I've watched the food channel with my mother a bunch of times. We don't need little squiggles of sauce decorating everything."

"Squiggles?" Her culinary school teachers would be horrified. But the teasing twinkle in his eyes helped ease her nervousness the way it usually did.

"People expect ranch stuff."

"Ranch food?"

"Yeah. Eggs for breakfast. Sandwiches and side salads for Saturday lunch. Fancier eggs and French toast or pancakes for Sunday brunch."

The menus she was used to cooking had been a lot more elaborate. "I can do all that. No problem."

"And no squiggles?"

"I promise. No squiggles."

"Good. Now for the next favor…" He grimaced as if not looking forward to asking this favor of her.

"You mean there's more?"

"Aunt Sharon is taking Dan's place as the wrangler on the guest ranch. She can't watch Gabe while she's with guests on a trail ride or doing other things to entertain them. And I can't take him with me most days."

"So…"

He swallowed hard. "So I'd need you to watch Gabe and do the cooking. That's a lot to ask, I know, and I'll understand if you say no. But—"

"Are you trying to talk me *out* of taking the job now?"

This new twist didn't make sense. As hard as he worked to not be near her, she knew he wasn't asking her to come because he wanted her there. Yet it sounded strange for someone so desperate to try to talk her out of helping him.

"No, uh…" He lost his battle to hold on to his hat, knocking it onto the floor. He straightened after retrieving it. "No, but I am asking a lot from you."

The frantic look in his eyes tugged at her heart more than it should. "If I can entertain three nephews or a niece under the age of eight at my apartment all weekend, I can watch one five-year-old."

"So you'll do it?"

This man who wanted only her friendship needed help. Help she could give. She couldn't let her past pain turn her into someone so selfish and calloused that she wouldn't help someone in need.

"Gabe's a sweet little guy. We should do great together." She marveled at how normal her voice sounded. Her heart was pounding so hard she wondered if Mac could hear it.

"Thanks, Rachel. This means more than I can say." Mac rubbed his hat across his leg. "One more thing before I forget. It's a guest ranch, so please wear jeans and cotton shirts. Something that looks a little Western, if you can."

"I'm not sure if most of my jeans or tops are what you have in mind."

"Our guests want a total Western experience. They won't expect to see you in a white outfit like the cooks wear on TV."

"You mean a chef's coat?" She fought to keep from laughing at him.

"Yeah." He shifted. "So could I ask another huge favor of you?"

"Sure, ask away." His pleading tone almost made her say yes without knowing what he wanted.

"Go shopping tomorrow morning for more jeans and Western shirts before I come to pick you up. I'll be happy to reimburse you for them, since you'll never wear them again."

"Sure. Which store around here will have what I need?"

"Tucker's Farm and Ranch Supply."

A half an hour later, he'd answered all the other questions she could think to ask, plus he'd offered her generous wages. And it seemed like he only had one ranch hand. So he sounded as if he'd be busy taking care of his ranch. His aunt would be the one spending time with the guests. Sharon would most likely be the Greer she saw most of the time.

He rose from the chair. "If you think of anything else you have questions about, call me. I'll stop by about eleven tomorrow morning, so we have time to get whatever food you want to buy."

Good thing the ranch menu wasn't extensive, from what she'd seen of the small grocery store here. But mentioning such a thing would make her sound like a big-city snob, so she'd remained silent.

"You don't have to take time away from your work to help me shop." He could reimburse her for the food, too.

"It'll be only for this week, so I can help you. Plus I'll let the store know to let you buy food on the ranch's account, so you can shop alone later."

Alone. One of her favorite words. The goal that had eluded her since coming to Sunrise.

"Okay." She stood, unable to think of anything more at the moment.

"I really appreciate your help, Rachel."

He grinned as he extended his hand to her. As his work-worn hand engulfed her fingers, his firm grip emphasized his simple words of gratitude.

"You're welcome." She stared into his warm brown eyes longer than she should.

She slid her fingers from his instead of giving in to the sudden crazy wish for him to keep holding her hand. "I'll see you tomorrow."

"Yeah, tomorrow."

Her heart sped up again as she walked him to the door. The tomorrow she'd just agreed to was one thing she'd never have dreamed of doing. Four to six weeks of tomorrows.

Could she really do this? And not get emotionally involved? Only time would tell…

Chapter Five

Mac hoisted Rachel's suitcase into the trunk of her shiny blue car. Rachel's Mustang was going to look as at home on a ranch as she would. Meaning, not at all.

She set a smaller bag next to the big one he'd loaded, leaving very little room for anything else. "That should do it for a few days." She shut the trunk.

More like a couple of weeks, if he was packing for himself, but he knew better than to say that out loud. Or to mention he had no idea why she needed two clear plastic bins full of shoes.

"Anything else?" Her small trunk wouldn't hold much more, so she'd be putting things in the back seat pretty soon.

"I'll put my herbs in after we get back from the grocery store. They'll get too hot in a closed-up car."

"Herbs?"

She nodded. "I have my own herb garden."

He looked over her shoulder at the sporty car with very little room left. "Better be a small garden."

He probably shouldn't have said that. What was it about her that made him say all the wrong things? Maybe because he couldn't help thinking all the wrong things about a big-city woman who shouldn't be so interesting. Alicia had grown up in Sunrise and still got tired of small-town life. Would Rachel last more than a few days around here?

"Um… Mac, are you still here?"

"Huh?"

Her lips turned up in too-cute smile. "Whatever's behind me must be fascinating, the way you're staring in that direction."

"Yeah, I'm here. It's hard not to think about business a lot, since I'm trying to do three people's jobs." He wouldn't tell her or anyone else what he'd really been thinking.

"My herbs are only a few clay pots that will fit on the floor of the back seat."

"Right. Our ranch garden wouldn't fit in a car."

Her face lit up. "You have a garden?"

"Mom and Aunt Sharon do. I'll tell you about it on our way to the store."

Talking about plants was a good way of preventing himself from saying something wrong. Again. From enjoying her bright smile. From enjoying watching her more than he should as he opened the door for her to get in his truck.

Except he needed to mention a thornier subject than plants. He glanced over as he pulled away from her grandmother's house.

"I couldn't say this with Miss Connie around, but my job offer is business only."

She nodded. "I understand."

He returned his attention to the street. Staring into her mesmerizing green eyes was dangerous. "I promise your grandmother and my aunt *won't* understand."

"As long as we do, that's all that matters. We'll be okay."

"Yeah, we will."

His growling stomach reminded him he hadn't taken time to eat much for breakfast so he could rush through chores. "Do you mind if we eat lunch somewhere before we go to the grocery store? I ate breakfast early."

He wished he could take back the words he'd just said almost instantly after saying them. He didn't want to eat lunch with Rachel. To be seen out alone with her anywhere. To give anyone in Sunrise the idea that they were more than friends or business associates. No one thought anything of him grocery shopping for the ranch, so they'd be good there. But anywhere else in town...

"I guess lunch would be good, since the afternoon will be so busy." The way she hesitated before answering eased his anxiety. Some.

"What would you like?"

"Burgers, since they're fast and close by."

"Sounds good to me." He turned off Miss Connie's street and headed toward the Burger Shack.

Rachel swallowed a groan as Mac held the door open for her at the only burger place in town. It was full of customers when they walked in. Several people smiled as they placed their orders. He insisted on paying for lunch. Rather than cause a scene, Rachel didn't challenge him.

All the effort they had made to convince everyone they were only friends looked to be going up in smoke faster than a kitchen in a grease fire. The last open table for two was in front of the window. By the front door.

Too many people looked their way and grinned. Not a single person in the friendly little town stopped by to say hi. Granna had gone to get her hair done yesterday. She probably couldn't resist mentioning they'd been to the Greer ranch on Saturday. Which, she feared, meant the townspeople all assumed Mac and Rachel wanted to be left alone.

Four to six weeks. She gritted her teeth to keep from saying the words out loud as she stirred her sweet tea. As quiet as Mac was, he might be thinking the same thing. Neither of them dawdled over the meal.

Rachel relaxed some when Mac parked in the grocery store's small lot. There were only two other cars. Wonderful.

"Aunt Sharon checked the pantry. She says there's not much flour or sugar left and to get whatever spices you'd like. Lisa had planned to restock today, but that didn't happen."

"Okay." He'd told her yesterday couples had already booked two of the three cabins and the third could yet be reserved, so she'd made a tentative grocery list after he'd left.

A list that would be longer than she'd thought if the pantry barely had staples. So much for making this a quick shopping trip with Mac. She ended up wandering slowly down each aisle, hoping she wouldn't forget something she'd need later.

When they reached the condiment aisle, Mac set a couple of bottles of barbecue sauce in the basket.

"We're out of sauce, too." He looked down at the cart instead of at her.

"You don't have to stay with me if you need to pick up other things for y'all to use at home." She'd use any excuse she could to not walk the entire store with him.

He shook his head. "This is for the ribs and brisket we'll smoke for Saturday night supper."

Ordinary bottled sauce wouldn't be on her menu for ribs and brisket. "I'll have plenty of time to make a homemade sauce if you'd like."

"You would?"

"Sure. Why not be as authentic as possible with an original ranch-made sauce?" A sauce that would complement the meat instead of drowning out the flavor.

"That's great, if you're sure you don't mind." He set the bottles back on the shelf.

"I'd love to."

His easy grin made her glad she'd spoken up. Her brothers had started calling her a food snob well before she finished culinary school, all of them completely unwilling to understand she'd discovered being a chef was her passion and calling.

Or had been, until her world had collapsed in one evening. Enough of that. She'd focus on this unexpected temporary job and see where it might take her. And stop focusing on things best left in the past.

An hour or so later, Mac loaded the food in the back seat of his double-cab truck. "So now we head back to get your car and herbs?"

"Right."

After Rachel had settled the clay pots in her car, Granna followed them outside. "Karen Thornton is coming by tomorrow, so don't worry about me. I called your father and aunt already to tell them I'll be fine."

"Good." Rachel grinned. Her supposedly helpless grandmother could still take charge. "I didn't want to be the one to convince them."

"They're more than convinced after I talked to them."

She hugged her grandmother goodbye. "I'll see you Sunday afternoon."

"All right, sugar." Granna waved from the front porch as Rachel backed her car out of the driveway to follow Mac to his ranch.

She spied two cars on the road as they left Sunrise. Nothing at all like rush-hour traffic in Dallas. She enjoyed her relaxing traffic-free drive until Mac turned onto a county road. Cows, mesquite, cedar and an occasional oak or pecan tree dotted pastureland that stretched to the horizon in every direction she could see.

Landmarks. Without Granna in the car telling her where to turn, she had to pay attention or she'd never find her way back to Sunrise. She grabbed her phone and activated the microphone. Recording everything she could see—every turn, every road number—was the only way she could think of to keep from getting lost if she wanted to go back to town alone.

Without Mac.

* * *

Mac drove under the wooden gate bearing the name of the ranch around four o'clock. Still Waters was a misnomer right now. The woman in the bright blue car behind him meant he'd have little peace for the next several weeks.

He bypassed the gravel driveway by the house and headed toward the guest ranch quarters. The groceries had to be put away, and Rachel probably wanted to unpack her things. Gabe and his dog bounded toward the truck. He halted to let them catch up. He leaned over to open the passenger door for his son.

"Come help me at the guest quarters?"

"Yes, sir." Gabe climbed up into the truck. "Can Peanut come, too?"

"I've got a lot of groceries in here. He can follow us on his own." Which the dog would do, since he and Gabe were inseparable pals.

Mac parked his truck in the gravel drive outside the guest dining room. Rachel pulled her car in behind him. Without waiting for Mac's help, Gabe scrambled out of his seat and headed straight for Rachel.

"Hi, Miss Rachel."

"Hi, Gabe."

The boy received the warmest smile Mac had seen her give anyone today. In fact, it was one of the few smiles he'd seen from her. Not that he minded she hadn't smiled like that at him. Especially since he'd never received the kind of smile that showed off the dimples he'd never noticed before. Didn't need to be noticing now. They were friends and business associates. No more.

"I've been waiting for you. Aunt Sharon said you'd be here soon." Gabe beamed at her.

"You have?" She turned her full attention to his son. Gabe nodded.

Rachel's eyes sparkled. "I have a few leftover chocolate chip cookies with me."

"Yum." He licked his lips.

"It's up to your dad when you can have them."

"After supper, buddy." Mac slid the ice chest from the back seat. "We need to get this stuff into the fridge."

The dog trotted up as Rachel reached for a bag of groceries. Peanut accepted a pat on his head from her before walking over to Gabe. The mutt never did that with someone he'd seen as little as Rachel. Never wagged his tail, either.

Gabe eyes lit up, and he tapped Rachel's arm. "Peanut remembers you."

She turned toward Gabe. "He's a nice-looking dog."

"He's my bestest friend." Gabe grinned. "He likes you, 'cause he let you pet him."

"He probably senses I like dogs." She smiled. "You can tell me about him while your dad and I put groceries away."

With every step she took back and forth, Gabe stayed at Rachel's side.

"Monnie named my dog, because he's the color of a peanut and kind of shaped like one."

"He calls my mom Monnie." Mac supplied information as he set the eggs in the fridge. "Mom's the one who put the kitchen together."

Rachel nodded before returning her attention to

Gabe and listening for more details about his four-legged friend.

"We don't know how many kinds of dogs he is, so Daddy says he's a mutt," Gabe chimed in, interrupting Mac's thoughts.

She set cans on the pantry shelf. "I had a dog like that when I was a kid. He was great."

"Peanut is the bestest dog ever."

The conversation went on as if Mac weren't there. She must be a terrific aunt. She obviously had spoken the truth when she said she wouldn't mind watching Gabe. His son would follow her anywhere as long as she gave him cookies or let him talk about his dog.

A dog that hadn't barked at her once. Who let her pet him. Peanut never took to people he'd only met once or twice.

She turned her attention back to Mac after the fridge and pantry were finally loaded up. "My things next?"

"Yes, ma'am."

She laughed. "You sound like you're talking to Granna. Rachel is fine."

"I'll remember that…ma'am."

Rachel laughed again.

He liked hearing her laugh. It made him smile. She'd done him a huge favor. Not many people would take on a new job on such short notice. But he couldn't go there. She'd be gone soon, and there was no way he could risk his heart again.

By the time they got Rachel's belongings up the stairs, his aunt had sent him a text to tell them supper would be ready soon.

"Did Aunt Sharon say what we're having?" Mac looked over at Gabe as the boy watched Rachel take her new jeans out of the plastic bag.

He shrugged. "I saw her get the Crockpot out."

"You've both been so much help. Go eat. I can take care of the rest of this myself." Rachel turned to unzip the big suitcase Mac had set on the bed.

"Aunt Sharon's text said she's fixed enough food for you, too."

"Oh." Her expression sobered.

He hoped her unenthusiastic response meant she still shared his thoughts about staying friends and business associates only.

"You're gonna eat with us, right, Miss Rachel?" Gabe's tone sounded more like begging than asking.

"Looks like I will." She smiled in his direction.

"You can follow us back to the house in your car, if you'd like. There's room to park it in the shed we built as a garage. It could stay there out overnight. It's just a quick walk back here." Mac edged toward the door.

"Thanks. I'll do that."

A few moments later, Aunt Sharon ushered them toward the dining room as soon as they walked inside. "I fixed pot roast with carrots and potatoes, since I wasn't sure how long y'all might need to get everything done."

"It smells delicious," Rachel said, as she breathed in the tempting smells filling the dining room.

Aunt Sharon glowed at the compliment. "I set a plate for you next to mine, if that's okay."

"Thanks."

Mac took his usual chair across from the women

and next to Gabe. Neither he nor his aunt felt comfortable taking the chairs at the ends of the table that his parents had used for years. For once he thanked God for a small family that only needed a table for six. A table just the right size to keep Aunt Sharon from seating Rachel next to him again, since she couldn't justify adding the extra leaf and chairs tonight.

"We have peach cobbler for dessert," Aunt Sharon said when they were finishing up, setting her napkin by her plate.

Rachel emptied her tea glass. "Thanks, but I can't eat another bite. I'll help you clean up while everyone else has dessert."

"I'll help Aunt Sharon clean up, so you can go back to your rooms and put your things up." Mac liked washing dishes about as much as cleaning the barn, but he needed Rachel to leave. Before he started having more thoughts about her that he shouldn't.

"But I hate to eat and run." She set her fork on her empty plate.

"We understand."

Mac ignored his aunt's raised eyebrows. She knew full well how he felt about helping with dirty dishes. But giving Rachel an excuse to put her things away would give his aunt less time to match him up romantically with their new ranch cook.

"It'll be dark soon. Maybe she shouldn't walk alone." Aunt Sharon glanced out the picture window.

"Peanut and I can go with her." Gabe gave Rachel an adoring look.

Aunt Sharon shook her head. "Only if your dad goes, too, in case the coyotes are out."

Rachel's eyes widened. "Coyotes?"

Mac worked to keep his expression serious. She wouldn't be happy with him if she knew he was chuckling on the inside. The woman was so completely out of her element.

"They usually don't come any closer than downstream from where we were Saturday night, but don't be surprised if you hear them." Looking into her pretty eyes, he wondered if they could get any bigger.

"How far downstream?"

She was way too cute when she got nervous. "A couple of miles or so from the dining room and cabins."

"We leave floodlights on all night, so we've never seen them up around the house, honey. But we like to be careful with a five-year-old around." Aunt Sharon's soothing tone was similar to the one she used to calm Gabe.

"Of course." Rachel didn't look as convinced as she sounded.

Half an hour later, Mac, Gabe and Peanut walked out the front door with Rachel. Yes, he had to be careful with his son, but Aunt Sharon had wasted no time using that as an excuse to keep him with Rachel a little while longer.

Let the matchmaking games begin.

Chapter Six

By the time Rachel went downstairs the next morning, sunlight was flooding through the large window over the sink. Whoever had designed the commercial kitchen loved natural light. The wide windowsill was the perfect size for holding six small pots of herbs. In Dallas, there were some condos in restored older buildings that might have similar features. Maybe she'd look into a place like this.

Wherever she ended up next, whatever she might be doing, she wouldn't repeat the mistakes she'd made the last two years. She didn't want another time-consuming job that took up too much of her life. Sorting out a couple of important things meant she was making some kind of progress.

She closed her eyes, willing her thoughts to return to the sunny, pleasant place she'd be working in for the next few weeks. Organizing the pantry was at the top of her list. She hadn't had time yesterday to decide on the best spots for everything.

Checking out the contents of the other cabinets and learning the whereabouts of cookware and dishes would come later. Sharon insisting Rachel eat supper with them last night had rattled her enough she hadn't thought to ask Mac to show her where everything was in the kitchen.

A knock on the back door interrupted her about an hour later.

"It's me, Rachel." Sharon's voice drifted through the door.

"And me." Gabe announced himself, too.

"The door's not locked. Come in."

What a silly-sounding comment to ranchers. Of course the door wasn't locked in a place like this. She set the last of the spices on the pantry shelf as they walked inside.

"Do you need any help with anything?" Sharon asked as she closed the door behind her and Gabe.

"Not so far."

"You're welcome to organize the kitchen the way you'd like. Caroline won't mind." Sharon's easy smile backed up her words.

"Caroline is Mac's mom?" She thought she remembered that from Mac's prayer requests at church.

"Yes. Let me know if you have any questions."

"I'm a real good helper." Gabe beamed as he looked up at Rachel.

"Yes, you are. You helped me and your dad a lot yesterday." In more ways than he'd ever realize. She'd much rather talk to him than Mac.

"Since everything's okay here, Gabe and I'll go clean

the cabins. Let's go, helper." Sharon patted Gabe's blond head before ushering him outside.

Blissful silence and solitude wrapped around Rachel like a comfortable throw on a cold day as she opened the island cabinet to check its contents. Professional cookware. A top-quality stand mixer with attachments. By the time she finished going through the kitchen, she'd developed an immense appreciation for Mac's mother.

Her first peek into the linen closet didn't disappoint, either. Place mats, table runners and simple centerpieces stocked the shelves. Everything needed to set a table for any season, all done in a rustic ranch theme with boots, horses or ropes for accents. Caroline Greer understood creating ambience as well as she must understand the need for a well-equipped kitchen. Setting up the dining room for guests would be fun.

Ranch-style cooking and serving looked much more doable after this morning. She'd overseen small company banquets of up to a hundred people. Cooking for six guests would be like going on vacation. She might survive this strange new environment better than she'd thought.

"Knock, knock." Sharon's greeting preceded her and Gabe into the kitchen. "We've finished getting the cabins ready. Want to see them while they're empty?"

"I'd like that." Rachel followed them out the back door.

The three cabins were a short walk from the dining room, with separate paths leading to each one. *Simple but not too rustic* was the best description Rachel could think of. The pairs of rocking chairs on each front porch looked inviting.

Sharon opened the door to the first cabin. "Caroline and Rodger went for a restful bed-and-breakfast approach, so there's only a bed and small sitting area with a table in each cabin."

"It looks nice."

Welcoming, like everything else she'd seen at Still Waters Ranch. Blue-and-red-print curtains on the east-facing windows on either side of the door. The bright quilt on the bed. The braided throw rug gracing the wood floor. The entire room beckoned people to relax and recharge.

"Me and Aunt Sharon are going 'sploring after Daddy comes in for lunch. Can you come eat with us?" Gabe's invitation interrupted Rachel's thoughts.

"I'd planned to set up the dining room."

She needed to get to know Gabe better, since he'd probably be with her a lot this coming weekend. But she'd find another way to do that while trying to avoid Mac.

"We've got plenty to share. Nothing fancy, just soup and sandwiches." Sharon turned off the lights as if she was sure Rachel would come with them.

"Thanks, but I bought some groceries for myself yesterday." Rachel intended to keep things as business-like as possible.

"Please come, Miss Rachel."

One look at Gabe's expectant, upturned face threatened to undo her resolve. "Why don't you come get me after lunch?"

The shine returned to his brown eyes. "Okay." He skipped out the door with his great aunt.

While enjoying her solitary lunch, Rachel congratulated herself. Avoiding Mac might be easier than she'd thought. Around one thirty, Gabe and Sharon came to get her.

Gabe, with Peanut at his side, trotted toward the large pecan tree shading the dining room and kitchen. "This is a good way to protect us from wolves." He handed a bent stick to Rachel.

"Wolves?"

He nodded. "Or bears."

"Not real ones." Sharon grinned as she looked over Gabe's head toward Rachel.

Her fear must be showing more than she wanted if Sharon saw through her so quickly.

"We can't see them, but they're real." He picked up a stick for himself. "This is a special wand. It makes us invisible."

"It does, huh?" The boy's imagination was amazing.

"Uh-huh. Then the bears and wolves can't see us."

He handed his great-aunt a stick, too, before scampering off again. "The ladybug left a message." He kicked a good-size piece of bark with the toe of his shoe. "See, I remembered not to pick it up first."

"That's good." Sharon looked over at Rachel while Gabe studied the bark in his hand. "Never pick up a rock, log or anything that size without kicking it over first to look for snakes or scorpions."

Rachel stopped in her tracks. "Scorpions? Snakes?"

Shivers radiated up her spine. They let a five-year-old go exploring in a place with snakes and scorpions? They protected him from evening coyotes just in case but let him wander almost at will in a snake-infested area that could also be crawling with scorpions.

Sharon nodded. "Most of the snakes are harmless, but we've got some copperheads and rattlesnakes."

"You do?" Rachel hoped she didn't sound as afraid as she was, but the high pitch of her voice betrayed her.

"Snakes don't like us any more than we like them, so as long as you're careful, you'll be okay."

"Right."

Wrong. She was far from okay. She hated scorpions. Snakes even more, harmless or not. Coyotes at night. Snakes and scorpions by day. Every story she'd heard on the news about snakebites or coyotes attacking joggers in town flashed through her mind. Not what she'd planned when she'd agreed to this new job.

"The bears took the rabbit. We have to rescue him." Gabe interrupted Rachel's fearful musings. "See, the ladybug wrote it all down."

Sharon waited for Gabe to finish looking over the message on the piece of bark. "Where's the rabbit?"

"In the bushes by the end of the driveway." He trotted off on his adventure.

"We don't let Gabe get in the bushes, just to be safe. Do I need to show you what poison oak and poison ivy look like?" Sharon trailed behind Gabe, leaving Rachel no option but to walk with her.

"Yes, I think it'd be a good idea for you to point out anything poisonous."

Sharon's eyes twinkled, but she didn't voice whatever she was thinking about Rachel's obvious discomfort and fear. Maybe her good manners kept her from laughing out loud at their city-born-and-raised chef.

Rachel squared her shoulders as she forced herself to put one foot in front of the other. One closed-toed shoe after the other. She'd save her sandals for going to town. Facing fears was the best way to deal with them, so she kept walking. Aware of her surroundings. Watchful of every step she took.

The irony of her situation was almost laughable. Almost. In Dallas, she'd always kept her eyes out for suspicious-seeming situations. Never gone for a walk alone without pepper spray. But she'd lived her life. Gone where she wanted to go. She'd do the same here. She wouldn't allow her fears to control her.

By the time they rescued the rabbit, Rachel had gotten in a good walk without seeing a single snake or getting too close to poison ivy. And maybe without giving away how uneasy she was about the normal dangers of nature she'd never had to think about.

She checked her watch. It was almost three o'clock. "I've got to get back to the dining room."

"Aww. Already?" Gabe's obvious disappointment was as cute as his high-boned cheeks.

She nodded. "I have to set things up for the guests coming in Friday."

"Okay. Can you 'splore with me again?"

"I'll have to see how much time my cooking takes first." She wouldn't make a promise she wasn't sure she could keep.

"I'll help so you have time."

Telling him no was impossible as soon as she looked into his wide brown eyes signaling his serious commitment to helping all he could. "We'll see what we can work out. Okay?"

He grinned. "I'll see you later, Miss Rachel."

"'Bye."

She headed in the direction of the dining room. In spite of her fears, she'd had a great time with Gabe. Another child she could enjoy without having one of her own. Her throat tightened as her heart rebelled against such thoughts.

No. Thinking about having children of her own someday meant loving and trusting a man again. That was a risk she wasn't willing to take.

Yet.

Mac laid a rack of ribs on the top shelf of the smoker while Gabe and Peanut romped nearby. Aunt Sharon had put the brisket on the bottom rack just before noon. The last cabin had been booked this morning. After exploring with Gabe, Rachel had been too busy the rest of the afternoon to eat supper with them. His aunt and Gabe had been disappointed. Not Mac.

Guests coming in by six tomorrow should keep Rachel busy the rest of the weekend. Their arrangement was working out great so far.

This evening he would spend time with Gabe. Time uninterrupted by matchmaking.

"Got a minute?" Rachel called from somewhere not far behind him.

He jumped. "Sure." Another time when good manners did not have anything good about them. He had other plans with his son.

Before turning toward her, he checked the temperature gauge and his attitude. Since she'd turned down his aunt's offer for supper with them, she must have a necessary reason for walking over here now.

"Hi, Miss Rachel." Gabe trotted toward her. "What's in the little bowls?"

"Sauce samples for the ribs and brisket." Her eyes sparkled, making it harder than it should be to look away from her.

"No cookies?"

She laughed. "Not this time. This is for your dad to taste and tell me what he thinks."

"Oh." Gabe skipped over to the slide on the side of his swing set.

Rachel turned her attention to Mac. He tried to focus on the bowls she carried instead of the disarming full-dimpled smile she gave him. She usually reserved those for Gabe. Something had her feeling cheerful. He couldn't recall hearing her laugh much since they'd first met.

"Setting up the dining room didn't take as long as I'd thought. So I've been experimenting with sauces. Want to be my taster?" She slipped a plastic sandwich bag with spoons from the pocket of her loose-fitting gray pants.

"I'm always ready for tasting something good."

As he refocused his thoughts on barbecue sauce instead of the woman who'd made it, he led the way to the wooden picnic table under the pecan tree.

She set the bowls on the table and took the bench on the other side of him. "The sweeter sauce is in the green bowl. The tangy one is in the blue." She took the plastic lids off, then pushed the bowls and spoons toward him.

He sampled the sauce in the green bowl. "Not too sweet, like some store-bought ones."

"Thank you."

The second sauce didn't disappoint, either. "Whatever you put in this one is perfect. Not too spicy, but just enough of a kick."

Her face lit up, reminding him of the way Gabe had looked when he'd found his much-loved teddy bear under the Christmas tree.

"I thought I'd make some of each, since some people don't like spicier sauces."

"Good idea. Either one of these beats the stuff I've been buying from the store." He licked the spoon he'd used to taste the spicy one. No, the tangy one, as she'd called it.

"I'll make more tomorrow while the bread rises."

She'd mentioned homemade dinner rolls for Sunday while they shopped for groceries. "You've got everything planned out if you're making stuff for Sunday on Friday."

She shook her head. "I'm baking bread tomorrow for sandwiches or breakfast toast."

"Wow. Nobody expects you to do that." He was surprised by her enthusiasm.

"Cooking is fun," she said, smiling.

He had no trouble believing her, since she sounded as excited as someone planning a dream vacation. Her

bright smile looked as if she'd just arrived at her desti-
nation. Maybe Aunt Sharon was right about this temporary job helping Rachel find her way back. If so,
he'd be glad to have a small part in making her happy.

The more glimpses he saw of the true Rachel, the
more he liked her. A woman who was sure to leave here
as soon as his parents returned.

A curtain moved in the kitchen window. Only an
inch or two. Aunt Sharon had to be watching them. In
spite of his troubling thoughts, a chuckle slipped out
before he could stop it.

"Did I say something funny?" Rachel's smile
dimmed. She sat with her back to the house, so she
had no idea what had caught his attention.

"Not you. My aunt. She's probably still looking out
the window, thinking I didn't see the curtain move just
enough for her to see us."

"Oh." She laughed.

A nice, soft laugh he wouldn't mind hearing again.

"Aunt Sharon wouldn't be happy to hear us talking
about sauces and homemade bread."

She shrugged. "I'm used to people not understand-
ing why I like talking about food."

"I like to eat, so I'm interested in food." Especially
if it meant they could keep this conversation centered
on things as impersonal as this.

"Good. I found a delicious-looking chicken-fried
steak recipe online. Would that work for the guests'
dinner sometime?"

"Oh, yeah. That sounds great."

Good thing Aunt Sharon wasn't out here with them.

She might mention how much Mac liked chicken-fried steak. The woman who loved evenings outside was staying in the house so he wouldn't have any choice but to be left alone with Rachel. His aunt had managed to matchmake even when she couldn't say a word.

Judging from the way the sun had dipped closer to the horizon, Rachel talked about meal ideas for a good thirty minutes or more. Mom was the only other person he knew who enjoyed food so much. He shoved away thoughts of how much his mother would like Rachel. Mom would have to get Rachel's email address if she wanted any of the recipes their temporary chef intended to try for the few weeks she'd be here.

Coyotes howled in the distance.

She stopped midsentence in her description of a delicious-sounding peach cobbler. "I didn't intend to stay this long."

"That's okay."

If not for looking toward the western horizon once in a while, he'd have lost track of the time, too. Watching the evening sun was safer than looking at her the entire time the way he wanted. The way he had no business wanting.

"Gabe, help me walk Miss Rachel back to her rooms?"

The words slipped out before he thought. She was a grown woman capable of walking alone for a mile. A woman who didn't want his company any more than he should want hers.

"Yes, sir." Gabe and Peanut bounded toward the table.

"Y'all don't have to do that. It's not dark yet." She

stacked the bowls neither of them had touched the last few minutes.

The way she gripped the plastic lids signaled she wasn't as brave as she sounded. Which made him want to walk with her more than he already did. He had no business wanting to protect a woman who wanted to return to a city he'd never want to live in.

"Me and Peanut can walk by you."

"I'd like that." Rachel grinned his direction as she rose.

"Daddy, you walk on the other side so Miss Rachel won't be scared." Gabe grabbed Rachel's free hand.

Rather than make a scene, he followed his son's instructions. Good thing she carried bowls in her other hand. If not, he'd have had to shove his hand in the pocket of his jeans to keep from reaching for hers.

"Miss Rachel's not really scared. She likes walking with you." He grinned at Gabe as he said the first thing he could think of to get his mind off how close Rachel was to him. How close she didn't need to be.

"Really?" Gabe looked up at her.

"Really." She squeezed his hand.

Mac's fingers itched to be where Gabe's were. He clenched them into a tight fist.

He had to remind himself that she'd be gone soon. Six weeks. Eight, max. It was easier on his heart if he could remember that.

Rachel halted when she and her escorts finally reached the short path leading to her rooms. "Good night. Thanks for walking me home."

"G'night, Miss Rachel."

Mac tipped his hat to her.

No matter how badly she wanted to run, she forced herself to walk at a normal pace to the dining room door. No just because of coyotes. Spending so much time with Mac was making her think about relationships again. Which was a dangerous road to travel.

Coyotes howled again as she closed the door. She flipped every light on. Anyone could tell the animals were a good distance from here. Yet they had rattled her again. She had to get used to them. To deal with this fear, too. This was the last night she'd let Mac and Gabe walk her back here.

The last night she'd talk to Mac until sundown. He'd listened to every word she'd said about her ideas for meals for the ranch guests, barely taking his eyes off her. No one in her family ever listened with such rapt attention while she talked about food or recipes.

She set the sauce bowls to soak in the sink. Mac's enthusiastic praise for her barbecue sauce experiments sent her thoughts in a more pleasant direction. He'd probably be glad to taste test her ideas for chicken-fried steak or peach cobbler, too.

But no, she'd aim to keep her relationship with Mac on a friendship basis. A business-only basis would be better. Safer. No matter how well he had listened to her.

By nine o'clock the next morning, she had vegetable-beef stew simmering in the two slow cookers she'd found in a cabinet. She'd love to thank Caroline Greer for setting up a kitchen so well. Maybe she'd get to meet the lady before returning to Dallas.

Next, she started the dough for the bread and let it rise. Two batches of barbecue sauce simmered on the stove by the time she put the bread in the oven. Sharon and Gabe came by a little before noon. She politely turned down their invitation to eat lunch with them.

She fixed a quick sandwich for herself around one o'clock but didn't take time to sit while she ate. The afternoon flew by while she made corn bread and apple pies.

Being so busy made her heart happy. She hadn't had such a pleasant day all to herself since she'd come to Sunrise to help Granna. Every dish was cooked to her specifications, with no one else interfering. She leaned against the kitchen island to survey her temporary domain of light wood cabinets and beige granite countertops. Too bad she wouldn't be able to find such a stress-free job in Dallas. Today had gone well enough to make her want to return to a kitchen. She could cook again. Create again.

But she was adamant that she never wanted to get too close to a man again. Cooking she was good at. Judging men and their motives…not so much. She'd stick with her strengths.

The alarm on her phone went off. Four o'clock. It was time to go upstairs and change into her ranch clothes. She touched up her makeup and brushed her hair. The sensible, short layered cut worked great on such a busy day. But she'd have to make an appointment with Granna's stylist pretty soon, unless she was planning on growing her hair long.

She surveyed her Western look in the dresser mirror

a few minutes later. The fitted shirt with cap sleeves looked a little like a chef's jacket. The blue gingham check trimmed with yellow piping didn't. The jeans were another definite change.

This new job was a change for the better if it helped her start over. She was already doing things she'd never thought she'd do in a place she'd never thought she'd be. Things didn't feel as scary as they had a month ago. The idea of making six people happy at supper tonight wasn't the least bit scary.

The scary part was when Mac ushered the guests into the dining room a few minutes before six. He looked much too nice in his good jeans. And his beige Western shirt couldn't disguise his broad chest, his strong muscles gained from working hard on the ranch all day.

The way his gaze zeroed in on her the instant he stepped inside made it hard for her to breathe. His shining eyes combined with his slight nod signaled his approval of her Western transformation.

Chapter Seven

After tucking Gabe into bed, Mac settled onto the couch to enjoy the rest of the Monday night Cowboys game. But thoughts of Rachel made it hard to concentrate on football. He'd seen her Saturday night at supper and at the campfire after that.

With a half dozen guests around, he'd been able to focus on how pretty she looked without anyone noticing. Or how natural, as if she belonged here on the ranch. Plus, Aunt Sharon hadn't managed to find a way for him and Rachel to spend one second alone.

He and Gabe had gone to church yesterday morning, leaving his aunt here to help Rachel with brunch. After the guests had left, Rachel had headed back to Sunrise, to her grandmother's house. Next Sunday, he'd insist on staying at the guest ranch with his aunt so Rachel could go to church. Gabe would have to miss church every other Sunday, but that couldn't be helped. The weekend had gone better than he'd hoped. The next few weeks might not be as stressful as he'd feared.

"Mac, you need to see this." Cell phone in hand, Aunt Sharon marched into the living room just as the Cowboys made it first and goal at the three-yard line.

"Can it wait till halftime?"

"This is important," she said, shoving her phone toward him. "Our first two-star review. The other two aren't much better."

"What?" He grabbed her phone to see for himself.

The couple from New York had loved the food, their cabin, the beautiful Hill Country scenery and especially the relaxing, welcoming atmosphere. They praised Aunt Sharon's expertise and friendly personality.

But apparently, a real Texas ranch boasting a genuine Western experience should have a cowboy host for trail riding and roping. Not a cowgirl. Thus, they had to give the two-star review. The next review was four stars but agreed they'd like to have seen a real cowboy before campfire time on Saturday. The three-and-a-half-star reviewer made similar comments.

Mac stared at the reviews silently. Then looked over at his aunt. "That's sexist and not fair at all. You grew up working this ranch. You're as genuine a cowhand as I am."

"True. But the couple from New York told me they're originally from England. So many Europeans I've met get their ideas of Texas ranches from TV or movies, so they left disappointed. Who knows about the others?" She shrugged.

He reread the reviews. "Maybe I should offer the New Yorkers a partial refund?"

A slow smile turned up his aunt's lips.

"What are you smiling about?"

He couldn't think of anything to be the least bit happy about. If other people wouldn't accept Aunt Sharon, he wasn't sure what the next step should be. He hated giving in to such people, but his bottom line didn't give him much choice.

"You take my place with the guests. Tim respects me. He'll be fine working the ranch with me on the weekends." Her silly grin spread ear to ear and sparkled up into her brown eyes.

"Maybe Tim would take your place if I explain how much we need him to do that." Mac grabbed onto the first thing he could think of to thwart her plan.

"You know he's not that good with people, even if you could talk him into it."

She had him there, and she knew it. Unless he could come up with another way to solve their problem. Another way to not work closely to Rachel. *Think, man. Think fast.*

"I could do the trail rides and roping demonstrations on Saturday. We could take turns helping Rachel on Sunday so one of us gets Gabe to church. The guests shouldn't mind a woman doing the local history talk while they walk the river after breakfast."

Her expression sobered. "We can try that as long as it doesn't get us another bad review. But we need to figure out a way for Rachel to make it to church every other Sunday."

"That's only fair. Any ideas?"

Letting his aunt come up with a solution could only mean more trouble for him. The way his aunt's face glowed signaled that her idea would be something else he wouldn't like.

"If the guests don't mind me telling them the local history, they won't mind me serving their Sunday breakfast, either. I can do that every other week so you and Rachel can go to church."

He shook his head. "You shouldn't have to do everything alone like that."

"I can manage it two or three times in the next few weeks or call a friend. Harry would help me."

"I'm sure he would." At this point he doubted Harry minded helping Aunt Sharon with anything at all.

"Are you that afraid of being with Rachel?" She looked straight into his eyes when she asked the question.

"I'm not afraid."

He was terrified. Rachel's all-in approach to this temporary job gave him more reasons to admire her. Making homemade bread and sauces from scratch was going way beyond what he'd expected. But he wasn't about to admit that to his aunt or anyone else.

She sighed. "Rachel won't be on the trail ride. She ride a horse, and she can't rope a fence post unless someone slips the rope over by hand. So you won't be with her much. You'll see to that."

The more his aunt goaded him, the more he wanted to prove her wrong. Except doing that would mean agreeing to her plan. But if he didn't prove her wrong, she'd keep badgering him. Keep shoving him and Rachel together unless they could work out a way to make his aunt's scheme backfire on her.

"I'll be happy to switch places with you and go to church the same Sundays Rachel does."

She paused on her way out of the room. "Now that we've solved that problem, enjoy the rest of the game."

That was next to impossible.

Everything had been upended. What he'd really like to do was give the sexist couple a piece of his mind, but that wouldn't solve any of their problems.

He glared at Sharon's back as she left the room. Knowing he'd stew over everything. She knew him too well. He'd do exactly as she'd predicted and see that he was with Rachel as little as possible. As soon as Rachel got here on Thursday, he'd show his aunt she was right.

No, he wouldn't. He and Rachel were friends. She'd proved her friendship by helping him out when he really needed it. He'd prove his friendship by...

The cheering on the TV drew his attention back to the game. But his mind went back to Rachel. Staying away from her as much as possible was absolutely necessary. No matter that he'd prove to Aunt Sharon how right she was about him and Rachel.

He could take his time tending to the horses after the Saturday trail ride. Long enough to miss seeing her at lunch. By the time he finished the roping demonstration, he'd have to clean up and start getting ready for supper.

With Aunt Sharon off working on the ranch with Tim, she'd never know how little he'd see of Rachel. Never know how right she was about her nephew. She would not succeed at putting him and Rachel together, no matter how hard she tried.

* * *

Rachel woke around seven Monday morning. Sleeping in felt great. Maybe she'd go for a walk in the park after breakfast.

But after her walk, then what? Granna's attic was the only unorganized spot left in her house. Today's forecast called for ninety-two degrees. Not the kind of late-September day to be up in an attic.

The smell of coffee drifted into her bedroom. Granna must already be in the kitchen. Time to start breakfast and another pleasant morning with her grandmother. Something she'd enjoy while she could.

With Rachel away four days in a row now, Granna would soon realize she needed to hire someone part-time to help her do the things she should no longer do. This unexpected job at the Still Waters guest ranch might accomplish the family's goal for her grandmother in a way they could never have planned.

"Good morning, sugar." Granna beamed at her when Rachel walked into the kitchen that had changed little since Rachel was a child.

"Good morning." Rachel accepted a kiss on her cheek. Something else she'd miss soon. "What are you hungry for?"

"One of your fluffy ham-and-cheese omelets." Granna poured herself a cup of coffee.

"Omelets it is."

Rachel headed toward the fridge. The well-stocked fridge, since Granna's friend Karen had gone with her to the grocery store while Rachel was working at the ranch. Another indication her time with her grandmother wouldn't last much longer.

"So what would you like to do today?" Rachel took the chair next to the end one her grandmother occupied.

"You can help me get ready for my next grand adventure."

"Your what?"

Granna popped a bite of eggs into her mouth and took her time chewing. "Delicious as usual."

"Granna, what kind of adventure?" Rachel stirred cream into her coffee as she waited for the answer her grandmother was more than happy taking her time to give.

"Remember I told you Karen's only sixty and can't afford to stay in her house after losing her husband to cancer last year?"

Rachel nodded. As usual, Granna hadn't spared the details of Karen's story. The woman's only child was a missionary in Argentina. Karen wanted to stay in Sunrise, since she had no other family. But Rachel couldn't see how all that could be connected to Granna.

"I've been praying about it. The answer to Karen's prayer could be the start of a new life for both of us."

"What do you mean?" Rachel had recently heard Karen mention in church how the Lord had helped her sell her house for a good price.

"Karen's closing on her house Wednesday and moving in with me on Thursday."

Rachel almost dropped her fork. "She is?"

"I get the help I need. Karen can stay in Sunrise. It's

perfect for both of us—and for you." Granna's smile spread from ear to ear.

"Really?" *How?* She swallowed the last question.

It wasn't the least bit perfect for her, as far as she could see. Granna had converted her third bedroom into a sewing room years ago. Where would Rachel stay when she came back from working at the ranch next Sunday?

"Absolutely perfect. With a private apartment at the ranch, you won't be in anyone's way out there. I'm sure Mac and Sharon won't mind if you move in for a few weeks." Granna's eyes sparkled.

Rachel choked back a groan. Too bad she hadn't been in church yesterday. Sharon and Granna must have had a fine time putting the finishing touches on Granna's grand adventure. Which would be a grand disaster for Rachel and Mac.

Too bad she'd given her word to help him out. Quitting wasn't an option. She didn't do that to friends. Especially since quitting would mean moving in with her parents.

Keeping her promise to Mac left her with only one option. Granna had all but literally shoved Rachel's back against a wall. More like shoved her out the door.

"I'll call Mac tonight after he's finished with work." Rather than try to think of more to add to the conversation, she took a bite of her suddenly tasteless omelet.

"Good. You can help me get your room ready for Karen. Pastor Leon and a couple of the deacons are coming tomorrow to move my guest room furniture to the attic and get Karen's bedroom set over here."

"Sounds like you've got everything under control."

Rachel hoped her fake smile looked as cheerful as her forced words sounded. Her world had spun completely out of control in a matter of minutes. Practically being evicted from Granna's house wasn't the way she'd planned to ease her way out of her life.

"As I said, it's perfect. Your dad and aunt thought so when I called them." Granna's triumphant grin contrasted completely with Rachel's feeling of doom.

"That's great."

Granna had sold the entire family on her grand adventure. And probably also turned them all into helpers for her grand matchmaking scheme to pair Rachel off with Mac.

As she finished eating the rest of her breakfast, Granna chattered on about how God had worked out all the details so quickly. Rachel forced down the rest of hers, saying only enough to try to keep up her facade of happiness about Granna's good fortune.

She made the dreaded call to Mac in the evening. Mac said she could move to the ranch tomorrow, if she wanted. He'd sounded about as enthusiastic as she felt. Then he'd asked if she'd come after seven so they could talk alone.

About what, she couldn't imagine. But all she knew was that staring into his warm eyes got harder and harder all the time.

These next few weeks would be more of a struggle than she would have ever imagined after their first awkward meeting. He had to remain only a friend. Only her boss. She'd be safe as long as she kept reminding herself not to make the same mistake twice, no matter how nice Mac was.

By Tuesday, the room Rachel had occupied for the last few weeks was ready for Karen's arrival. A little before seven thirty, she drove under the wooden arch to Still Waters Ranch. Her heart and mind were anything but still. She texted Mac to let him know she was here. His message asked her to pick him up at the house. He wanted to help carry her things upstairs.

"I've got something for you." He grinned as he slid into the passenger seat.

"You do?"

He patted the green metal cylinder in his other hand. "An LED lantern, in case you're out on the ranch after dark. You can see where you're going and not trip. No coyote will want to come near this."

"Thank you." The thought of wild animals and creatures on the ranch still bothered her. It was nice to know he'd picked up on that and thought of this solution.

Half an hour later, Rachel surveyed the bed, which was almost covered by two suitcases, a garment bag and clear plastic shoe boxes. "Thanks for your help."

"You're welcome." He brushed a strand of brown hair from his eyes.

Coyotes howled in the distance. She managed not to flinch.

"Looks like you're getting used to them." Mac grinned.

Not as used to them as he thought, but he'd be less likely to walk with her places at night if he assumed the coyotes didn't bother her now. Not having an escort should make her much happier than it did.

His grin disappeared. "I know you want to put your clothes away, but I'd like to talk to you first."

"Sure."

Still trying to figure out what he needed to say to her with no one else around, she followed him down the stairs to the dining room.

"I could tell when you called last night that Miss Connie surprised you with her new living arrangements." He pulled out a chair for her before he seated himself across from her at one of the small guest tables.

She nodded. "More like shocked."

"Yeah. Neither of us planned for this to happen." He paused as he looked into her eyes.

His intense gaze made her wonder if he was thinking more than he was saying. He looked so serious. As if whatever he wanted to say meant a great deal.

"Since you were forced to come live here, I understand if you want to go back to Dallas as soon as you can."

"I keep my promises. Dallas can wait a few more weeks." She'd always been loyal to friends. And this friend needed her help more than anyone had in a long time.

"Thanks. I appreciate that."

"You're welcome." She willed her hands to stay in front of her on the table instead of reaching over to touch his arm. He had no idea how much she valued his consideration of her feelings. Giving her an out to leave here after being practically trapped into staying on the ranch by her grandmother.

"Before I forget, I got a ranch credit card in your

name so you can buy groceries without me tagging along." He reached into his shirt pocket and handed her the card.

"Thanks. I'll probably go buy food tomorrow afternoon."

"Good idea. All three cabins are already booked for this weekend."

"Wonderful. We should both be too busy for your aunt to try to match us up."

"That'll be harder to avoid now, actually." Mac shifted in his chair.

"What? Why?"

"Remember the New York couple originally from England?"

"Yes."

"Well, they gave us a two-star review."

"They did? That's odd, since they were very friendly around me."

"Right. But they said they expected a cowboy, not Aunt Sharon, on the trail ride and such."

"That's crazy. And so wrong."

He nodded. "Exactly what I think. But Aunt Sharon doesn't want to risk any more reviews like that."

"What are you going to do?"

Mac explained the new arrangement he and Sharon had worked out, then added, "They all loved your food. One lady called it 'gourmet ranch.'"

Rachel blushed. "I've never heard that before."

"Yeah." He shifted in his chair. "Switching with my aunt on Saturdays might be okay. I can probably stay busy enough with guests to not be in your way much until supper. But Sundays could be a problem."

"How so?"

The worry lines on his face reassured her he still wanted to keep his distance. The way he leaned in closer from his side of the table didn't. His mixed signals unnerved her.

"Because I'll be the one doing the history walk with the guests and seeing they get checked out okay every other Sunday."

"Maybe I can spend extra time cleaning the dining room and kitchen. We'll think of something to stay away from each other."

"That might work. But we'll be going to church together every other Sunday, even if we take our own vehicles."

"We will?"

He nodded. "Aunt Sharon insists she can handle everything herself. I think she's just looking for an excuse to ask her friend Harry to help her." He paused as he took in a deep breath. "So you and I get to go to church the same week."

"They are too good, your aunt and my grandmother. And Granna probably has my entire family's blessing to try to pair us off."

"I've always liked rooting for the underdog. Looks like that's what both of us are." His wry-looking grin sent her thoughts in the wrong direction. His smiles were more disarming by the day.

"That's the truth." He folded one arm over the other as he leaned in again.

Worse, he stared straight into her eyes. She found she couldn't look away. He looked so good. Now that she'd be staying at the ranch full-time, how was she supposed to not appreciate how good-looking Mac was?

"I should put my clothes away." She scooted her chair back.

He stood.

"Thanks for helping me get all my stuff upstairs."

"You're welcome. Good night, Rachel."

"Good night, Mac. I'll do my best not to see you tomorrow."

"Yeah. I'll do my best, too." He headed for the door.

She forced herself not to see him out. Not to think about looking at the stars with him.

Not to think about spending more time with someone as thoughtful and handsome as him.

Chapter Eight

With nothing to do but drive to Sunrise for groceries later on, Rachel took her time with breakfast the next morning. The sun streamed through the east window of the little kitchen as if to welcome her back. Two squirrels romped in the branches of the big pecan tree shading the apartment. They were happy, contented-looking creatures who knew exactly what they were doing. Where they were going.

So unlike her.

She sighed. She still had no idea what direction her life would take. Would she move back to Dallas? Stay in Sunrise?

She picked up the Bible she'd carried in from the bedroom. She'd been so sure she had God's blessing on her life, her choices. How could she have been so wrong? She turned to the Psalms, one of her favorite places to look for answers.

Her phone chimed, signaling a text. She checked the screen. It was Sharon wanting to know if Rachel needed help with anything. And Gabe wanted her to eat lunch with them later.

Rachel thanked Sharon for asking about her. She hated to disappoint Gabe, but she planned to leave in an hour or so to eat lunch with Granna, then buy groceries for the guest ranch kitchen. So she'd be gone for much of the afternoon.

A string of ladybugs and smiley face emojis, followed by a question mark, was the majority of Sharon's reply. She finished the message by saying Gabe hoped Rachel could come explore with him tomorrow.

Rachel didn't have the heart to tell Gabe no. Snakes or no snakes, they'd go exploring tomorrow morning. Gabe would be so happy to be with her that he probably wouldn't notice her fear of snakes. Getting ready for guests could wait until Thursday afternoon.

Which meant she'd better use the rest of the time she had this morning to finish putting her things away. First she'd text Granna to tell her when she'd stop by so her grandmother would be ready to go to lunch with her.

But her grandmother begged off lunch until next week. Too many people were coming in and out of her house today for her know when her lunch time might happen. It seemed Granna was doing fine without Rachel's help.

As close to eleven as she could manage, Rachel drove her car toward town. She'd grab a snack at the grocery store rather than be at the ranch when Mac came in for lunch.

On the way to the grocer's, she drove past Donita's Hair and Nail Emporium. She should make an appointment for a haircut, since she'd be here a few more weeks. She pulled her car into a nearby spot, then walked in.

"What can I do for you?" Donita tossed a cape into a plastic bin.

"I'd like to set up a time for a haircut."

"Would now work? I had a highlight cancel, so I have time."

"That would be great."

She wasn't crazy about grocery shopping with pieces of hair still clinging to her shirt or scratching her neck. But getting a haircut without making a special trip to town would work.

After Donita finished, Rachel made a quick trip by Granna's house.

"Hi, sugar." Granna beamed as Rachel walked in. "I really like your hair with the shorter layers. You must have made an appointment with Donita."

"Yes, ma'am. She had a cancellation, so she could get to me."

"I've always been happy with her." Granna led the way to the living room. "The men just finished moving my furniture to the attic. They went to Karen's house to get her things."

Rachel settled onto the couch with Granna, glad for this time to visit. "Good. I think you and Karen will do great together."

"So do I. Have you had lunch yet? We could go to the Morning Glory after all."

"Thanks, but no. I hadn't planned on taking so much time for a haircut. I need to get back to the ranch in time to start making a meat sauce this afternoon."

"Sounds like you're busy."

"All three cabins are already booked."

"That's wonderful." Granna patted Rachel's arm. "You look happy."

"I'm glad to be cooking again."

"I knew you wouldn't be able to give that up. God has given me a new path. Keep listening to Him so you'll know where He's guiding you."

"I will." And she would. She had no desire to repeat her past mistakes.

After visiting with Granna a little while longer, she left and headed to the store. Her food shopping for the ranch kitchen went faster this week without Mac along. She parked her car in front of her welcoming little ranch apartment around four thirty.

Her timing was excellent. Today couldn't have been planned better if she'd tried. If Sharon offered an invitation to supper, Rachel could honestly turn her down. She needed to start the barbecue sauce for the brisket and ribs, so she'd have time to keep her promise to Gabe and go exploring tomorrow morning. Giving in to her fears would only disappoint her little friend.

The stars were coming out by the time she finished all her prep and had created the sauces. She'd wait until tomorrow to put her car in the garage close to Mac's house. No need to have him walk her back here because of coyotes. Or give him any idea she wasn't as brave as she'd pretended to be lately.

She grinned to herself as she loaded the dishwasher. She'd managed to avoid Mac all day. Which, she soon realized, didn't feel as good as it was supposed to.

Thursday morning, she went exploring the ranch with Gabe and Peanut while Sharon cleaned the cabins. The ladybug sent them on a couple of adventures. Gabe didn't appear to notice how carefully she watched every step she took around any bushes, rocks or logs. If not for possible snake or scorpion sightings, roaming the countryside on a clear day was something she would have never anticipated.

"I'm hungry, Miss Rachel." Gabe grabbed her hand. "Aunt Sharon says you're s'posed to eat with us."

One look into his innocent eyes meant Rachel didn't have the heart to tell him no.

Sharon's face lit up when Rachel and Gabe walked into the kitchen. "Did y'all have fun roaming around the ranch?"

"Yes, ma'am."

"Good. Go wash your hands. We'll eat when your dad comes in."

Gabe marched off to clean up.

"Thanks for watching him this morning." Sharon set soup bowls on the table.

"You're welcome. Can I help with anything?"

"No. We're just waiting for Mac."

A few minutes later, he walked in the door. If seeing Rachel surprised him, he didn't show it.

Gabe told his dad all about the giant squirrel he and Rachel had rescued from the bad wolves. Again, the little boy's constant chattering kept her or Mac from having to say much to each other.

After finishing his sweet tea, Mac scooted his chair back. "Gotta get back to work. I'll see y'all at supper."

Not Rachel. She'd told everyone how much she had to do to get ready for guests.

She kept her promise to avoid Mac as much as possible. She didn't see him again until he brought the ranch guests to the dining room Friday evening.

"Hope y'all are hungry. We've got the best chef in the business." Mac stood back to allow the couples to enter.

He stared at her much longer than he should. Because she couldn't help but return his gaze, she noticed him. He kept looking her way as she showed the couples where the buffet line started, not leaving until everyone had filled their plates.

On Saturday, Mac had to take care of the horses after the trail ride. By the time he walked into the dining room to grab something to eat, Rachel was busy cleaning up from lunch.

"Miss Rachel says I'm her 'sistant, 'cause I'm the bestest helper." Gabe beamed as he cleared the silverware off a table.

"That's good, buddy. You do whatever Miss Rachel says."

Gabe nodded.

"There's plenty of ham and cheese left over if you want a sandwich," Rachel told him as she stacked dirty plates in the plastic dish bin to carry them out.

"Thanks, I'd like that." Mac followed them to the kitchen.

Instead of rushing off, he took his time with his lunch, as if savoring every bite. He kept glancing up from his sandwich at her, which made her blush.

"I gots all the pepper and salt shakers." Gabe returned with his little hands full of the last set. He set the shakers on the counter by the sink for her to wash.

"Thanks. You're doing a great job."

"I can help you every day." The little boy's sunny personality and warm smile reaching all the way to his happy eyes melted Rachel's heart, just the way it had all day.

"Not tomorrow." Mac emptied his tea glass. "We're going to church."

"It's okay. I'll help Miss Rachel after church."

"I'm going to church tomorrow, too." She wiped the granite countertop with a wet cloth.

"With us?" Gabe's grin broadened.

"Probably not, buddy. Miss Rachel wants to see her grandmother. Maybe go out to eat with her and visit some after church."

"Can we eat out? I want chicken strips and French fries." Gabe turned his full attention to his dad.

"How about hamburgers for a change?" Mac rose.

Rachel concentrated on cleaning the salt shaker in her hand instead of the man standing a few feet away. Mac preferred burgers to going to the Morning Glory Café, where he knew Granna would want to go. Such a thing shouldn't disappoint her, but it did. Which meant she should want Mac to go anywhere but the café for lunch tomorrow.

Gabe shook his head. "They don't have chicken strips there."

"They have corn dogs. You like those. We should go someplace else for a change."

"But I like chicken strips, Dad."

The boy's disappointment hung in the air like a thick fog. Mac let out his breath, as if he could feel his son's unhappiness as well as Rachel could. No matter how much she didn't want to be with Mac, she couldn't bear to disappoint her little helper.

"Don't stay away from the café because I'll be there." She looked over Gabe's head into Mac's eyes.

Mac nodded. "Okay. Chicken strips and French fries tomorrow."

"Yay!" Gabe clapped his hands.

Rachel gripped the wet cloth to keep from clapping, too. She hoped she didn't look as happy as she felt.

Mac seated Gabe between himself and Rachel at the round table for five. Too bad a square one for four wasn't available. One look at Miss Connie seated across from him made him wonder if she wasn't happier about eating at the café than Gabe.

"From what Sharon says, your guests seem to love Rachel's cooking," Miss Connie said, not bothering to open the menu in front of her.

"Yes, ma'am. She's helping us get nothing but four- and five-star reviews. We're all glad she came to work at Still Waters Ranch." Mac looked over the menu he knew by heart, hoping the conversation would take a different turn soon.

"I'm *so* happy." Gabe launched into a detailed version of how he helped Miss Rachel.

Mac wanted to hug his son. Neither he nor Rachel were able to get in more than two or three words apiece before they placed their orders. Before the waitress could get away, Gabe announced that he was Miss Rachel's special 'sistant. Maria gave him an indulgent smile before heading toward the kitchen.

Without Aunt Sharon's help, Miss Connie had a harder time steering the conversation to things concerning Mac and her granddaughter. Maybe his aunt's idea to have him and Rachel off work on the same Sunday was backfiring on her and Miss Connie.

"How is everything?" Lance asked while everyone started eating. His gaze rested on Rachel longer than anyone else.

"Delicious as usual, Lance." Miss Connie paused from cutting up her pork chop.

Rachel nodded as she continued chewing a bite of salmon.

"My chicken strips are the bestest." Gabe dipped the last piece into his ranch dressing before popping the big bite in his mouth.

"Glad y'all like everything." Lance smiled then walked toward the next table.

Mac was way too happy to see the man leave. Any man with eyes in his head would notice such a pretty woman like Rachel. Lance paying attention to someone who was only a friend shouldn't bother him. But it did.

"You're good mosquito repellant, Malachi Greer," Miss Connie said. The mischievous twinkle in the older lady's eyes reminded him of a kid who had just pulled off a terrific prank.

"Ma'am?" He had no idea what she meant. No idea why she'd used his full name.

"I'll let my granddaughter explain later when y'all have time to talk, just the two of you."

The matchmaking pro was at it again, doing her best to set them up. Rachel looked down as she wiped her mouth with her napkin. He wouldn't admit it to anyone, especially not Miss Connie, but his curiosity about her words already had him thinking about asking Rachel for an explanation the next time they were alone.

Mac and Gabe got home, where he made his son change into play clothes. Then he went to check on Aunt Sharon while Gabe romped with his dog. Mac found her loading the dishwasher in the guest ranch kitchen with her friend Harry wiping down the countertops nearby.

"How did it go? Looks like you called in some reinforcements."

"Wonderful. Rachel is so good at prepping things ahead of time. Breakfast and lunch were no problem. That woman is amazing. The guests raved about the food."

"That's good." Rachel *was* amazing, but he knew better than to say as much out loud to his aunt or Harry. "Need some help?"

"I'll let you finish cleaning up the dining room tables. Harry and I have plans later this afternoon." Her bright smile reminded him of a teenager talking about a date with the most popular guy in school.

"Sure." He grabbed the other bottle of cleaning solution and another wet rag.

The less he said, the better off he'd be. Hinting that Aunt Sharon and Harry might be getting serious about each other wouldn't do. She'd use that as a chance to try to push him closer to Rachel. He was already having enough trouble reminding his heart to listen to his head about a woman who'd go back to Dallas sooner or later.

Rachel drove up in her blue Mustang around six. He and Gabe were in the backyard, where he had a good view of the garage where she parked. He knew because he'd been watching for her while playing with his son. More than a perfect early-October day had called him outside. Satisfying his curiosity about Miss Connie's mosquito comment had gotten the best of him all afternoon.

The only thing he'd repelled at lunch had been Lance. He might have done Miss Connie's bidding for her by keeping the café owner from having anything to do with Rachel. But allowing Lance to bother her was out of the question. So much so that he couldn't keep himself from listening for her car to drive up, to be sure the only person she'd seen after lunch had been her grandmother.

He had no business trying to find out that kind of information. Instead he should be running into the house to answer the phone or something. Any excuse to get away from her would be better than what he was doing now.

"Hi, Miss Rachel." Gabe waved to her as soon as she stepped out of the garage.

She waved back. Peanut trotted over to her, wagging his tail as if she was a long-lost friend. Gabe followed close behind. Mac wasn't the only one interested in this woman. He had to be careful. For his and Gabe's sake. So he joined his son and the dog.

"Aunt Sharon said we gots leftovers from lunch in the 'frigerator. Plenty for you, too."

"You had chicken for lunch, so you might want to save today's leftovers for a night when your aunt is too busy to cook."

"Please, Miss Rachel. Come taste the apple cake me and Aunt Sharon made the other day. It's almost all gone."

Rachel looked down at the little boy. "Then I'll eat with you tonight."

"Yippee." Gabe clapped his hands.

"Is it okay if I go change clothes first?" Rachel turned her attention to Mac.

"Sure." Although she looked fine in the green print dress that brought out her eyes. "That'll give me time to heat the chicken in the oven."

Rachel turned to walk toward her apartment.

His son went back to his swing set while Mac went to heat supper. About the time everything was ready to eat, Rachel followed Gabe inside.

He had to remind himself that she was here only because Gabe had begged her to come. Making his son happy was good. Except he suspected Aunt Sharon had put the idea of sharing leftovers and cake with Rachel in Gabe's head.

While they ate together, she didn't mention a word about lunch or her grandmother's comment about mosquitoes. He managed not to bring the subject up, either.

"Time for cake now?" Gabe licked his fingers after eating the last bite of chicken on his plate. "Can I give Miss Rachel her piece?"

"Use your napkin first."

Gabe grabbed his napkin, then crumpled it on the table next to his plate. "Now?"

Mac shook his head at his eager son. "I want coffee with my dessert." He spoke out of habit before thinking about it. He turned his attention to Rachel. "Would you like some?"

She nodded.

Glad to have an excuse to walk away from her for a short time, Mac started the coffee maker. Gabe pushed his yellow stool up to the counter. He reached for the cake stored in a plastic container.

"Let me get that, buddy. You can carry Miss Rachel's piece to her after I cut it."

Gabe didn't budge until the coffee finished and Mac cut a piece of cake for Rachel. "Use both hands to carry it."

The little boy nodded, watching his step as if he carried china instead of a paper plate. "Aunt Sharon says it's squishy 'cause of all the apples. This is Daddy's favorite cake." Gabe beamed as he set the cake in front of Rachel.

"I love any kind of Bundt cake." She gave Gabe a full-dimpled smile.

Mac set their coffee mugs on the table. He took his chair after cutting pieces of cake for himself and Gabe.

"This is delicious. I'd like the recipe." She looked to be savoring every bite.

"I'll tell Aunt Sharon."

Gabe wasted no time finishing his cake, then asked, "Can I watch a movie before bedtime?"

"A short one after I clean up in here. Then it'll be time for bed."

"I can do that, since you fixed everything." Rachel set her mug on the table.

Mac shook his head. "Throwing away paper plates and putting up leftovers won't take long."

"I don't mind so Gabe can have a little more time for his movie."

"All right." Mac soon settled Gabe in the living room with his favorite animated movie. Rachel had cleared the table by the time he returned to the kitchen.

"Do you want to save the two last pieces of chicken for Gabe?"

He nodded, then grabbed a plastic storage container from the cabinet. "Thanks for the help." He reached for the coffee decanter. Two cups left. A good host wouldn't finish it off alone. "Want to help me finish this so I don't have to throw out good coffee?"

"Sure." She handed him her coffee mug.

He hoped the only reason she was so willing to stick around was to maybe explain what her grandmother had mentioned to him. Not to let him know she'd spent some time with Lance after Mac and Gabe left. He leaned against the countertop, hoping to look as relaxed and uninterested as possible. She chose a spot a few feet away by the new cooktop his mom was so proud of.

"Your grandmother would be thrilled right now." So would his aunt.

"She did her best to set us up at lunch by insisting I should explain what she said." She looked down to stir her coffee.

"So what did she mean?" He hoped he didn't sound as eager to hear the answer as he was.

"I told her a while back that Lance is as annoying as a mosquito buzzing in my ear. He's nice and means well, but he treats me as if I'm some kind of celebrity since he found out I'd worked at a well-known restaurant in Dallas."

"And you don't like that?"

"Not really. He reminds me of a teenager with a crush on a singer. I'm just me. Nobody special."

No, she wasn't. Yet her lack of interest in Lance warmed him better than any amount of coffee on the coldest winter day. Standing in the kitchen talking to her felt natural. She looked natural, relaxed. As if she belonged here with him, sipping coffee and talking over something as silly as mosquitoes.

"Your real name is Malachi?"

He nodded. "Malachi Owen Greer. I'm named for my granddad."

"I like it. Family traditions are nice."

What was truly nice was the woman he couldn't quit looking at while they finished their coffee.

The coyotes started their usual howling. She didn't jump.

"I'd better head to my rooms." She set her cup in the sink.

"Want me to walk you over there, since you didn't bring your lantern?"

She shook her head as she started toward the door. "It's not quite dark, and I'm getting used to them. Good night."

"Good night."

As she hurried away from the house, he watched from the window. Her wide eyes had signaled she wasn't as used to coyotes as she'd boasted, but he'd let her walk back alone.

The coyotes were too far away to bother her. And he couldn't allow himself to become so comfortable with Rachel. She'd looked and acted as if she'd been feeling the same way.

He was thankful for coyotes.

Chapter Nine

Rachel parked her car in front of Granna's house in town, glad they could go to lunch this week.

"Hi, sugar." Granna kissed Rachel's cheek seconds after she stepped inside.

She relished it before returning her grandmother's hug. "Ready to go to lunch?"

"Oh, yes. I've got a hankering for hamburgers today." She grabbed her purse from the entryway table.

"You do?"

"I am. Plus I thought you'd enjoy lunch better without a certain pesky mosquito bothering you."

Rachel chuckled to herself. "Lance is harmless."

"Let's get hamburgers anyway."

"If that's what you want." Rachel followed Granna to the garage.

"It is." She grinned as she handed Rachel the keys to her old Camry. "You've set your sights on the best man. No use wasting time with another one."

"I'm not interested in Mac or any other man." Rachel backed the car onto the street.

"Sugar, my old eyes know what they see when y'all are together."

Rachel didn't bother contradicting her grandmother as she headed the car toward the Burger Shack. It was no use wasting her breath. Granna had seen only what she wanted to see.

"You know the old saying about one bad apple spoiling the whole bunch?" Granna looked over at her.

"Yes, ma'am." She welcomed the change in subject even though she had no idea why her grandmother had done it.

"That old saying isn't always true. Not every man is a bad apple. Look at Gramps, your dad, your uncle, your brothers. I could go on…"

Rachel was glad she didn't, sure the next man she'd name would be Mac.

"You take a chance on being hurt in a car accident every time you get behind the wheel, but you're still driving." Granna sighed.

"Mac and I are too different." She kept her gaze focused on the few cars around her. "Neither of us would be happy living where the other one wants to be. Maybe I'll try dating again once I get back to Dallas and finish sorting things out."

The truth of the matter was that she had no intentions of trying again with any man in the near future. And that was something Granna didn't want to hear.

In a few weeks, she'd go back to Dallas and make a fresh start. She wanted to cook again, but there would be no more sixty-hour weeks. She'd be sure to make time for her family, especially her nephews and niece. Time for herself to listen to God the way she'd been doing at the ranch. No time for making another mistake with any man.

"I pray for you every day, sugar." Granna interrupted Rachel's thoughts.

"I know, and I appreciate it."

She parked the car in front of the burger place. Getting here before the lunch-hour rush made it easier to find a good spot. Plus, it couldn't hurt for the regulars coming in to see her with Granna instead of Mac. Let everyone see Rachel had a life of her own apart from the ranch.

The Burger Shack sign grabbed Rachel's attention as she held the door open. "Granna, see the simple apron the cook on the sign is wearing?"

Her grandmother nodded as they stepped inside.

"Is there someplace in Sunrise where I could find an apron like that?"

"Mmm." Granna paused on her way to the counter. "Maybe Berman's Hardware. They carry grills and things to go with them. Why?"

"Let's place our orders, and I'll tell you." The idea the sign had given Rachel warmed her heart, giving her a good way to set aside the awkward conversation in the car.

They found a table for two not far from the door. Today Rachel didn't care who saw her here.

"I need an apron for Gabe so my little assistant stays cleaner."

"Good idea, but I don't think you'll find one in his size." Granna squeezed lemon into her water.

"Could you show me how to cut an adult one down for him?"

"That shouldn't be too hard. My new machine does embroidery. I could put his name on it, too."

"He'd love that." She could already picture Gabe's delighted smile. Granna's burger craving was paying off in ways Rachel never could have planned.

They finished their meal, then headed to the hardware store. When she spotted the aprons she wanted, Rachel could barely contain her happiness. "These are perfect. I'll get him a red one and a blue one."

Granna looked almost as thrilled as Rachel. "If you're not in a hurry to buy groceries, we could start on this as soon as you take me home."

"I can do that."

Why Granna was now fine with Rachel taking her time getting back to the ranch didn't make sense, but she wouldn't waste the opportunity to spend extra time with her grandmother, plus start a project that would make a little boy so happy.

Rachel got back to the ranch later that afternoon with groceries filling her small trunk and a Gabe-size red apron resting on the passenger seat. Granna had worked all afternoon to finish it while Rachel gone shopping. She parked in the driveway close to the house.

This was the perfect time to give Gabe his apron. Mac was most likely still working, so she'd drop off her gift and be gone before he came back to the house for supper.

She knocked on the back door, since Sharon was most likely in the kitchen fixing supper.

"Come in, Rachel. I didn't expect you, but we've got plenty to share." Sharon ushered Rachel inside as soon as she opened the door.

"Thanks, but I wanted to drop this off for Gabe. Then I have a trunk full of groceries to put in the fridge and freezer." Rachel held up the apron. "What do you think?"

"It's adorable. He's in the living room watching TV." Sharon called out, "Gabe, come in here. Miss Rachel has something for you."

Gabe and Peanut trotted into the kitchen. "Hi."

"Hi to you. I thought the best assistant ever should have his own apron." She held it out to him.

"Wow!" He halted in front of her as he stared wide-eyed at her gift. "For me?"

"For you. Want to try it on?"

"Yes, ma'am."

"It has your name on the front, too." Rachel slipped the loop over his head, then tied the straps around his waist.

"What do you tell Miss Rachel?" Sharon grinned at the beaming little boy.

He wrapped his arms around Rachel's waist. "Thank you."

"You're welcome. Thank my grandmother when you see her Sunday. She did most of the work. I only helped her a little."

"Okay."

"I have a lot of groceries to take care of. I'll see you

later, assistant." Rachel let herself out of the house before Sharon could offer another invitation to dinner.

After putting everything away, she fixed herself a simple meal. In spite of the tough conversation she'd had with Granna, her day had ended as close to perfectly as she could ever want. Making Gabe happy. Doing all her shopping. And avoiding time with Mac.

To celebrate, she treated herself to a walk. No use wasting a perfect fall day when a long-sleeve shirt was all she needed to be comfortable outside. She'd read somewhere snakes were less active in cooler weather. As long as that was true, she'd be fine. She'd take the lantern Mac had given her just in case she decided to watch the sunset.

His thoughtfulness was nice. Even better was that he'd given her a way to keep from walking with him once the coyotes came out. She wasn't as used to the noisy animals as she'd led him to believe. But she'd be fine walking back to her rooms with such a bright lantern.

She soaked in the peaceful quiet as she walked. Birds singing. No noisy vehicles or horns. A cottontail rabbit darted in front of her before disappearing into the evening shadows. As the shadows lengthened, she took the path to Longhorn Creek. She wouldn't have the luxury of enjoying such a place in Dallas. Better take advantage of it while she could.

The sun's yellow, purple and pink rays darted between wispy clouds as they painted the sky. She leaned against the back of the wooden bench. Maybe she'd make sure that her next apartment was close to a park. But no park in Dallas would ever be this quiet. This peaceful. This soothing. She breathed in the refreshing scents of trees and grass as the water rushed over the rocks. Water flowing home to the Colorado River.

Home. She needed to find where that was. Her next job wouldn't be so all-consuming that she came home only to sleep a few hours, then start another hectic shift. She'd be more careful this time not to let a job take over her life.

In case Rachel was upstairs in her rooms, Mac knocked hard enough on the dining room door to make it rattle. He waited. No answer. He pounded on it again. Absolute silence.

He grabbed the key from his pocket. If she'd replied to the text he'd sent about forty minutes ago, he wouldn't be doing this. She always answered texts. As promptly as possible. Even the ones from his aunt that she didn't want to see. This wasn't like her. A woman who still feared coyotes would be inside with the sun going down in half an hour.

A man with any sense wouldn't be standing here wondering where she was because he hadn't heard from her in forty minutes.

"Rachel?" He called her name as soon as he stepped inside.

Silence.

He took the stairs to her rooms two at a time. He knocked on her door. He called her name loud enough for her to hear. Knocked again. Nothing. He yelled again before inserting the key in her door lock. Still no response. No sign of her as he looked around the small living room. Her cell phone sat on the arm of the couch. That's why she hadn't responded to him.

But where was she? Somewhere close by, he hoped. She wasn't as used to coyotes as she pretended. He searched the rest of the little apartment just in case.

No Rachel. No lantern, either, unless she'd put it in a closet. Which he doubted she'd do, since she'd been so thankful to get it. Nosy or not, he checked both bedroom closets. No lantern.

So maybe she was getting brave enough to go for a walk alone? But where?

Think, man. You're being ridiculous. She had to be close by. She hadn't been at the ranch long enough to go anywhere without a definite marked path or trail. Such a sensible woman wouldn't strike out someplace she might get turned around or lost.

Longhorn Creek? He'd try that first, since the path down there was easy enough for a child to follow in the dark. He marched in that direction. He'd run if not for the risk of catching his boot on a tree root or something. His mom tripping like that had been bad enough. No use risking his neck.

As he went, he clamped his mouth shut to keep from calling her name. If she was close enough to hear him, he didn't want her to have any idea how anxious he was to find her and be sure she was okay.

Good friends watched out for each other. Panicking because he couldn't locate her was outrageous. If he wasn't careful, his heart would be in more danger than a man cornered by an angry bull. He slowed his steps.

The remaining rays from the setting sun shone on her

honey-brown hair and narrow shoulders as he entered the clearing. She looked beautiful, even from behind. His boots slowed. His pulse sped up.

"Rachel?"

She jumped.

"Sorry to scare you. I came looking for you when you didn't return my text." He walked up to the bench.

She stuck her hand in the pocket of the baggy pants he hated. "Oh. I must have left my phone at…in my room."

Had she started to say she'd left her phone at home? That couldn't be. His imagination was overreacting again. A city woman would never consider this place home.

"Yeah. You must have." He wasn't about to admit how he'd rushed into her rooms to see about her. "Um, I wanted to thank you for Gabe's apron."

Grinning, she scooted over to the end of the bench. "Your aunt says this is one of your favorite spots. I'll share, unless you want to be alone awhile."

He accepted her invitation, taking the other end as he'd done the first time they came here. Except this time, he itched to be next to her.

"You made Gabe's day. We had to make him take his apron off to eat so he wouldn't get it dirty before he comes to help you."

"I'm glad he likes it so much."

"I didn't expect you to go so above and beyond when I asked you to watch him."

"I don't mind. He's a great kid." She kept her gaze focused straight ahead.

"So the coyotes don't bother you anymore?"

She shook her head. "But I brought the lantern you gave me."

"Good idea. Better to see where you're going if you plan on staying out here much longer."

"I think I will. You're welcome to stay if you'd like. Nothing wrong with underdogs sticking together." She turned to look at him.

It was too bad that the light was dimming, so he couldn't see her dimples. "I'll stay. Don't tell my aunt. She knows I came to thank you, but…"

She laughed. "But she'd be much too happy to know we're here together."

"Yeah." He was much happier than he should be right now. Too relieved to see she was all right. Too impressed at how she'd braved a walk here in spite of her fear of coyotes.

He pretended to concentrate on the last rays of the sun the way she looked to be doing. The first time they'd come here, they'd stayed until the stars came out. Not tonight. He didn't dare.

"I'd better be sure Gabe gets his bath. He's at the stage where he's more allergic to water and soap than dirt." He chuckled as he stood up.

"I have a nephew like that."

"Good night." He tipped his hat to her.

"Good night."

She didn't budge from her spot on the bench. He walked away as fast as he dared on the darkening path. She could stay and enjoy the stars.

He had to leave before he gave in to the impulse to stay longer and talk with her.

Time alone with her was dangerous.

Chapter Ten

Mac jumped up onto the tailgate of his truck to eat lunch. Watching birds land on a cedar tree was a better idea than watching Rachel as closely as he'd done last night sitting with her at the creek. No, not better. But safer.

"With all the hay we've got in, you should be in good shape for winter." Tim grabbed the sack lunch he'd brought from home before sitting next to Mac.

"Yeah. We should be."

Especially since Rachel wouldn't be around then, but he'd keep those thoughts to himself. He'd known Tim ever since they were kids and knew better than to say anything about her to this old family friend. Tim was great at helping him out on the ranch while Dad was gone, but the man wasn't good at keeping secrets. Just the opposite, in fact. And there were already too many people trying to pair him off with Rachel. He didn't need one more.

He bit into his ham sandwich. Not as good as the ones with Rachel's homemade bread.

"You're too quiet. Something on your mind?" Tim took time out from his own lunch to look Mac in the eyes.

"I'll be glad when Mom and Dad get back."

"Yeah. Good thing Sharon could come for a while. And from what I hear, Miss Connie's granddaughter has been a big help, too."

"They both have." He finished off his sandwich, still missing Rachel's fresh bread. But that was all he dared miss. "We've had steady bookings for the guest cabins, so that should help us through the winter, too."

"Great. I had my doubts about a Dallas woman working as a cook or anything else out here. I've never seen her in church with a hair out of place. Know what I mean?"

"No, I don't." His insides bristled at the tone of Tim's voice.

Tim shrugged. "My wife says she hasn't seen the woman wear the same pair of shoes more than twice. Always has her makeup perfect. Not your usual ranch-type woman."

"The woman's name is Rachel. She's a chef, and she's working out great."

Mac didn't bother to curb his sharp tone. Neither Tim nor his wife had any right to criticize Rachel. But he couldn't defend her too much without everyone thinking he wanted more than friendship with her.

"Guess we'd better finish checking fences so we can move cattle to this pasture tomorrow," Tim said as he crumpled up the empty paper bag from his lunch.

"Yeah." Mac hopped to the ground, more than ready

to finish work today. He closed the tailgate as Tim headed toward the passenger side of the truck.

If Tim and his wife were saying such things about Rachel, he couldn't help wondering what others might be saying about her. Everyone in Sunrise knew how she had come to town to help Miss Connie. By now they had to know how Rachel had stepped in to help him out at Still Waters. Anyone with any sense would realize what a kind, unselfish person she was.

Anyone who didn't… No, he wouldn't be the one to set them straight. Miss Connie could do that with no trouble. And would, if she had any inkling of what Tim and his wife were thinking.

He didn't mind the way Rachel dressed. How she could look magazine-ready after cooking all day was amazing to him. A sure sign of how professional she was at her job.

It was *not* a good sign that he was paying such close attention to her. She was still a woman who'd be back in Dallas in a few weeks, but she also seemed as if she belonged here. From what Aunt Sharon said, Rachel was terrified of snakes and scorpions. But she went exploring with Gabe. And she'd braved the walk to Longhorn Creek yesterday in spite of her fear of coyotes.

Last night, he'd been in such a hurry to get away from her that he hadn't asked her why she'd come. Maybe he should have. She wouldn't have gone to the creek if she didn't like being there.

Maybe it was good he didn't ask. If she'd said she enjoyed the view or had come there to think, he wasn't sure he wanted to hear that. Not that his favorite place to unwind was becoming one of her special places, too. They already had more in common than he wanted to admit.

"You ready to get back to work?" Hand on the door handle, Tim stared at him.

Mac jumped. How long had he been standing here? He trotted to the driver's side. He had to get a hold of himself. Had to quit thinking about Rachel.

Tim had the good sense not to mention her the rest of the afternoon. Which didn't keep Mac's mind from wandering to thoughts of a woman he had no business thinking about. An honest woman who didn't hide her plans to leave here. So keeping his promise to himself not to ever risk loving someone again made perfect sense when it came to Rachel. Convincing his heart to be sensible got harder every time he was near her.

He walked in the back door late that evening, bone tired. They'd found a fallen tree on a fence line, causing them more work than they'd planned to repair that section. Better to find something like that this afternoon than when Aunt Sharon was out there helping Tim.

"You look worn-out. I'll heat your supper while you clean up," Sharon said.

"Thanks." He headed upstairs. If not for his growling stomach, he'd settle for a snack, then clean up and spend a little time with Gabe before going to bed early.

Just as Mac took a bite of chicken, Gabe walked into the kitchen, waving a sheet of paper. He plopped down in the chair next to Mac.

"I drawed a picture for Miss Rachel. See?"

Mac nodded while he chewed.

"This is me helping Miss Rachel." He pointed to two stick figures. The smaller one, dressed in Gabe's version of his prized red apron.

"That's really good."

"I'm gonna give it to her tonight." Gabe's smile spread ear to ear.

"Better wait till tomorrow. She might be busy now." Mac took a long swig of his sweet tea.

"She should be here soon with dessert." Aunt Sharon's eyes sparkled as she turned to grab a coffee filter from the cabinet. "She asked if she could come over after supper. She needs tasters for a new bread pudding recipe."

While chewing his corn bread, he digested the implications of what he'd heard. Rachel had called his aunt. She'd never done that before. Rachel getting comfortable enough on the ranch that she went for an evening walk with her trusty lantern was one thing. Getting so comfortable she invited herself over to their house was completely different.

Aunt Sharon started the coffee brewing. As usual, she looked much too happy about Rachel coming over. He tried to just focus on eating the rest of his supper. But even his appetite was ready to betray him. He shouldn't want another bite. He should be thinking of an excuse to leave so Gabe and Aunt Sharon were the only ones around when Rachel stopped by.

But he realized he was looking forward to seeing Rachel walk inside. As long as she didn't want more than opinions on her new bread pudding recipe, he'd be okay. So would she.

A light knock on the back door interrupted his thoughts. Gabe trotted over to let Rachel in. She carried her lantern and a pan full of something that smelled good enough to make his stomach growl again. The way she looked in her rust-colored shirt made him eager to see her.

"Can I taste it first?" Gabe followed her, inhaling the sweet aroma as she went in the kitchen.

"Sure thing, Gabe." Rachel beamed at him as she set the pan on the counter.

"If your bread pudding tastes as good as it smells, you'd better make a big pan for the guests tomorrow night," Aunt Sharon declared as she set plates and coffee mugs next to the pan.

Rachel's broad smile revealed the dimples he liked more every time he saw them. He concentrated on stacking his empty glass on his plate and carrying them to the sink. All she wanted was opinions on a dessert. Nothing more. He'd survive this taste test, too.

"You have to sit down so Miss Rachel can give you some pudding." Mac pointed to Gabe's chair. The little guy hadn't left her side since she'd come in.

Rachel served them all before taking a chair at the kitchen table. The too-small table for four. The dining room table would be better. No such thing as not sitting too close to Rachel with an aunt who was always sure the only proper chair for her was the one closest to Mac.

"I drawed a picture for you, Miss Rachel." Gabe held the paper he'd left on the table out toward her.

"You did?" She looked over Gabe's drawing while

the rest of them took their first bites of bread pudding. "You're a good artist."

The little guy glowed with pride.

For the next half hour or so, Mac let his son and aunt handle most of the conversation. Being exhausted gave him a truthful excuse for not saying much. It would have given him a good excuse to leave a few minutes after Rachel came. But he didn't. He stayed until Rachel decided it was time for her to go.

Rachel's new recipe was delicious. He had honestly complimented her on that. What he couldn't be honest about was how much she looked as if she belonged here in this house, with his family. Her relaxed posture and smile seemed to signal how much she'd liked being here, too.

This was heading into dangerous territory, and Mac wasn't at all sure what to do next.

Rachel gazed out her kitchen window, watching the squirrels play on the grass. She had stew in the slow cookers. Corn bread cooling. Bread pudding in the oven. Last night's taste test had been a huge success, so the guests coming in soon should like her new recipe, too.

She closed her eyes and let the rays of the afternoon sun wash over her. She hadn't been this happy, this content, in so long. Her next apartment would never have the views she had here, but it would be more conveniently located for family to visit her. For her to go see them. No more shoving aside loved ones for the sake of a job that had taken over her life.

Her friendship with Mac felt right, comfortable now. She was at ease around a man who meant it when he said he only wanted to be friends and business associates. Who appreciated her helping him out.

Her phone alarm dinged. Time to go upstairs and change. She checked her hair in the dresser mirror after buttoning her green-and-blue-plaid shirt. This weekend outfit felt normal now. She'd forgotten how comfortable a pair of good-fitting jeans could be. She'd forgotten a lot of important things before coming to the Still Waters Ranch. Things she wouldn't forget when she went back to Dallas.

Mac soon ushered in the weekend guests. "This is Rachel, the best chef around. She'll see you're well fed. I'll see y'all in the morning. Enjoy your stay at Still Waters." He left almost as quickly as he'd come.

Mac's hurried exit was the perfect way remind her that's all she wanted, too. She turned her attention to her job. She had guests to serve and new names to learn. She couldn't fill bowls with hot stew while concentrating on her boss. The best chef around had to live up to his praise, not spill food on her clothes.

"I'm no expert, but Still Waters is an unusual name for a ranch." A guest smiled as she handed him his bowl. "How'd it get that name?"

Rachel told them a brief version of Mac's story. Good thing no one asked her anything else about the ranch. She knew next to nothing about raising the beef that had gone into the stew she fixed every Friday.

Saturday kept to its usual routine—Gabe came over

as she was cleaning up from breakfast, so Mac could get ready for the trail ride.

"You put my picture on the 'frigerator?" Gabe's smile lit up his face.

"Your great-aunt gave me a magnet so I could put it up and look at it every day." She'd miss her little assistant when she left. "Want to help me clean tables?" Better to focus on the present than the uncertain future she'd have to face in a few weeks.

"Yes, ma'am."

Her usual Saturday chores and tasks kept Rachel and her helper busy. Mac came in long enough to grab a quick sandwich while she and Gabe cleaned up from the noon meal.

"Thanks for lunch. I never realized how much better a sandwich tastes with homemade bread. No wonder we've had all five-star reviews lately." Mac halted on his way to the back door.

"You're welcome." His simple, sincere compliment warmed her as if she was soaking in the rays of the afternoon sun. Nice how he noticed her efforts.

"I'll see y'all at supper." He tipped his hat to her and Gabe before heading outside.

Another quick exit she didn't mind. She also didn't mind his gentlemanly gesture of tipping his hat to her. A cowboy with old-fashioned manners was nice. No one in Dallas would treat her this way.

By the time she finished cleaning up from supper, Rachel was tired enough to sit quietly by the campfire and let Mac, Sharon and the guests supply the conversation. She'd rather ask ranching questions after the others had left. Since she and Mac would be working while Sharon and Gabe went to church tomorrow, she should be able to find out anything she wanted to know then.

Thinking about working alone with him didn't bother her now. She glanced over at him as the firelight flickered across his face. He looked more relaxed than any other time his aunt had tried to seat him next to her. They could be friends. Good enough friends to be comfortable with each other.

Not long after eight, the guests went to their cabins. Rachel didn't mind, since the crisp air and slight breeze made her wish she'd grabbed something warmer than a long-sleeve shirt to layer over her top.

Mac started dousing the fire. Rachel folded her chair, then grabbed one a guest had used. Their working partnership had reached the point neither of them had to talk about what needed to be done. Nice to be so at ease with each other. Scary if she wasn't careful to keep things between them strictly business.

"Time to head home and get ready for bed. Your dad can tuck you in in a little bit." Sharon interrupted Rachel's thoughts as she held out her hand to Gabe, who hadn't budged from his chair.

"Can't we stay a little longer?"

"You need to wash up. Go on." Mac motioned for Gabe to follow his great-aunt.

"Look! A falling star." Gabe halted as he pointed toward the southern sky.

Rachel looked up just in time. The entire night sky was beginning to sparkle as stars came out. "You don't see stars like this in Dallas."

"They don't have stars in Dallas?" Gabe stared up at her. Shadows obscured his face, but his incredulous tone left no doubt how baffled he was by her remark.

"We've got stars, all right, but we have so many lights in the big city they make it hard to see the stars."

"Oh."

"I have to come to Granna's house to see them. My brothers and I used to lie on our backs in my grandparents' backyard and look up at the sky during the summer."

"That's fun. Me and Peanut chase lightning bugs in the summer, too." He dodged his aunt's efforts to grab his arm.

"I can't see those in Dallas, either."

"Why would you live someplace you can't see stars or lightning bugs?" His eyes she couldn't see well were probably full of question marks.

"Well, because…"

Because Dallas offered things she couldn't find here. Four-star restaurants, museums, shopping. There was no need to worry about coyotes or snakes in Dallas, either. But how did she explain that to a little boy growing up in a place like this?

"Time to get ready for bed." Sharon snagged Gabe's arm and turned him toward home.

The boy's innocent question about why anyone would live in Dallas wouldn't let her alone the rest of the night. She wanted to go back to the big city. She'd miss the stars, the open country and this welcoming ranch, but a big city was the only home she'd ever known.

She turned out her light. Instead of crawling into bed,

she walked over to her window and parted the curtains enough to look out. Stars sparkled as moonlight created its own shining path across the yard. She should take a few pictures of the things she'd come to love and admire about Still Waters Ranch.

The photo she snapped with her phone didn't come out as clearly as she wanted, since she took it through the glass. Some night when she didn't have to be up at five the next morning, she'd take her good camera outside and get pictures.

Suddenly moved by the moment, she got her camera from the closet shelf, grabbed her lantern and headed downstairs. Snakes weren't out on cool nights, according to what she'd read.

She snapped a few pictures of the half-moon illuminating everything around her. She'd take more another night during a full moon. On another night when the cabins were empty and she could roam around without bothering anyone. The kitchen blocked the guests' view of this part of the yard, so she could come out in her pajamas and take pictures on a whim.

Guests or no guests, she'd never be able to do this in Dallas. Never would have mustered the courage to do this if she'd stayed there. Venturing into the unknown could be a good thing.

Chapter Eleven

The moon and stars still shone through her window when she woke Sunday morning. She'd forgotten to completely close the curtains. A quick look outside was all she had time to enjoy before starting her day.

But fixing brunch for six was nothing like the rush she'd had prepping for Sunday brunch at her old job. Personally filling everyone's plates as they filed by the serving table was another plus. She liked the direct interaction with people. Liked hearing what they thought of her recipes.

Mac came into the dining room not long before everyone finished eating. "If y'all haven't been there already, you're welcome to take the path down to Longhorn Creek. I'll be happy to come along and tell you a few tales about this area."

The couples soon left to walk, pitch horseshoes or whatever else they wanted to do with their morning. Rachel cleared tables without the help of her talkative little assistant. She'd gotten so used to Gabe being around, it seemed strange not to see the little boy, teddy bear in hand, walk into the room.

When Mac took the chair next to hers at lunch, she really missed Gabe. Friends could have lunch together. Especially a business lunch.

Except the streaming sunshine glinting off his broad shoulders sent her thoughts in very unbusinesslike directions. This cowboy was a genuinely kind man who appreciated everything she'd done to help his guest ranch. Appreciated her help with Gabe. Appreciated her.

Just so his regard for her didn't become more than friendship, since that's all either of them wanted. All she'd better want, if she wanted to be safe and not risk being wrong about him.

"Best chicken-fried steak I've ever had. I'll never be able to eat this at the Morning Glory Café again." The sparkle in his warm eyes emphasized his compliment.

She said the first thing she could think of to turn the conversation away from herself. "Home-grown beef doesn't hurt."

He nodded as he chewed another bite.

Mac stayed in the dining room to help guests check out after the meal. His place by the door was convenient for the guests, but not for Rachel. Trying not to watch him slowed down her efforts to clear the tables.

"Thank y'all for coming. We'd appreciate it if you fill out the opinion cards in your cabins before you leave." Mac held the door open for Collin and Beth Reese, the last couple to leave.

"We already did." Beth tossed her husband a mischievous smile. "We had a suggestion."

Collin looked down at the card he slipped from his shirt pocket. "You should marry your chef. Anyone with eyes can see that the two of you seem happiest whenever you're together."

Mac swallowed hard. Rachel froze as she struggled not to drop the pan full of dishes she held.

Finally, after several moments of silence, Mac just nodded and ushered them out the door.

The thin smile he tossed in Rachel's direction confused her. The look of longing in his brown eyes was just as confusing.

She hoped her forced smile didn't look too unnatural. The second the door closed behind the couple, Rachel bolted toward the kitchen. Her hands shook as she set the pan on the counter.

The couple's words about her and Mac jolted her. She did enjoy Mac's company. But she was adamantly against any entanglements or romantic attachments.

"Those people are worse than my aunt and your grandmother," Mac said, hovering in the doorway.

She jerked open the dishwasher with more force than she intended. "I'm glad all they asked me was how the ranch got its name."

"Yeah."

"If they'd asked anything else, I'd have been in trouble. Maybe you could tell me more about ranching in case someone wants to know more?" Ranching was a much safer subject than their relationship—or lack of it. She concentrated on loading dishes to keep from looking over at him.

"What would you like to know?"

She shrugged. Whatever he could tell her to keep her mind off the Reeses' suggestion sounded much better than it should before she started talking some sense into herself. "Whatever you think I should know to make y'all look good."

Mac sucked in air as she put the bowls on the top shelf of the dishwasher. Rachel made the ranch look good—no, *great*—without knowing a thing about cattle. Good thing she had her back to him and couldn't see how he could barely keep his eyes off her. Or see how the Reeses' suggestion about marrying her rattled him so much—because his crazy heart had agreed. Good thing he'd come to his senses and shooed them out the door.

"The best way to learn about ranching is to go for a trail ride." The routine words he'd told guests so often slipped out before he could even think about it.

"You mean...on a horse?" Her eyes looked huge as she whirled to look at him.

He swallowed his laugh. She looked even prettier when she was surprised. Which meant he probably needed to figure out a way to take back his offer before she accepted. Before he put his heart in more danger than it was already in.

"I've never ridden a horse before."

"Want to try?"

She looked up at him for a few seconds, as if thinking about his idea. He should be hoping she was thinking of a polite way to turn him down. But he wasn't.

"If we have time. When are Sharon and Gabe coming home?"

"Probably around or after four. She and Harry want to spend some time together."

"Right."

"I'll go saddle some horses for us while you finish in here. Meet me at the corral when you're through." He forced himself to walk away at a normal pace.

He didn't want to play games with her. But he'd do his best on the entire ride not to let Rachel guess how much he wanted to be with her. How he liked the idea of showing her places that meant so much to him.

Too soon, she stood next to him in the barn, staring at the sorrel mare he'd saddled for her. "I have no idea what to do."

"Mount from her left side."

"How?"

"Like this." He swung up into his saddle to demonstrate.

She grabbed the saddle horn. "What if I lose my balance? You make it look so easy."

He dismounted. "I'll stand by to help. How's that?"

In spite of her nerves, she did a decent job of getting up in the saddle. He adjusted her stirrups.

"If your knees start hurting while we're riding, the stirrups are too short. Keep the reins even on both sides, in line with the horse's head."

"Okay." Her death grip on the saddle horn signaled she wasn't the least bit okay.

"This little sorrel is gentle and used to greenhorns, like all our horses."

"What's a sorrel?"

"A chestnut or brown horse."

"I hope I don't make a fool of myself."

"You won't."

He might, however. He was the one in real danger of being foolish. Her willingness to try things she'd never done was yet another thing he liked about her.

For the next hour or so, she asked questions about the history of the ranch, about what he did to work it. Intelligent questions from someone who had lived in the city all her life.

"So you're as much a land manager as cattle raiser these days?" She looked over at him as they rode back toward the barn.

"Yeah. Moving cows from one pasture to the other helps prevent overgrazing. Mesquite trees use up a lot of water, so we try to control them." He reined in his horse as they finally reached the corral.

She copied him. "Now, how do I get off?"

He dismounted. "Want me to help you?"

"Maybe you should." She pivoted to grin at him as soon as both feet successfully touched the ground.

And lost her balance. A combination of crazy emotions and instinct kicked in, and he caught her.

Her wide eyes stared up at him, but she didn't pull away. And then he drew her closer and kissed her, unable to resist. She kissed him in return.

This couldn't be happening. He released her, stepping back the way he ought to have done sooner. "I'm sorry."

She shook her head. "No apology needed."

"You didn't sign on for this."

"No, but…" Her eyes had a look of wonder. Maybe like him, she still couldn't believe what had just happened.

"I didn't plan for this to happen."

"Neither did I, but maybe we should think and pray about where we go from here?" Her eyes were filled with questions.

This conversation shouldn't be going in such a direction. But his heart was all in. "You really want to do that?"

She blushed and asked, "Do you?"

"Yeah. Actually, I do." He shouldn't be saying any such thing. Worse, he shouldn't be thinking about kissing her again.

But he did. And she kissed him back. A gentle kiss. The kind that made his heart thud wildly in his chest.

A slow smile played across her beautiful face as she took a step back. "Yes. I think so, too. Let's see what happens."

"I should go take care of the horses right now."

She nodded. "I should go unload the dishwasher."

Once his common sense kicked in, he grabbed the horses' reins, then walked with them to the barn. Away from her. He couldn't think straight as long as he was looking at Rachel. She wanted to see what happened between them. So did he. But she was still a city woman who was planning to move back to Dallas soon. That might cause him all kinds of trouble.

But he realized that was the kind of trouble his heart no longer wanted to avoid.

Chapter Twelve

"Higher, Miss Rachel. Daddy pushes me all the way to the top." Gabe pumped his legs with all his might to make the swing go as high as possible.

"Your dad is stronger than I am, kiddo." She shoved Gabe as hard as she could.

He laughed. "You did it."

"Yes, I did." No wonder Mac had Gabe's swing set so well anchored. The little boy was fearless when it came to how high he liked to swing.

"Do it again."

"A few more times, then you'll have to slide or play with Peanut. I'm sure I can't push you as long as your dad does."

"I really wanted to go with Aunt Sharon to see Monnie and Granddaddy. I cried when Daddy said I couldn't."

"You'll see Monnie and Granddaddy real soon," she said, trying to soothe him.

Quickly changing the subject, Gabe said, "Know what?"

"What?" She gave him another push.

"I'm just *so* happy you're here, Miss Rachel. You make me feel all better."

"I'm glad."

When she'd told Mac they'd see how things might go, she'd had no idea they'd have three days to be an almost family, just the three of them. That Sharon would decide with no notice to leave this morning to visit with Mac's parents in Fort Worth and not come back until Wednesday evening.

"Woo-hoo!" Gabe squealed as Rachel sent the swing to the top again. "You're the bestest. Monnie and Aunt Sharon can't push like you do."

"I'm sure they can't."

After a few more pushes, Rachel's arms were tiring. "I need a rest now."

"Okay." When the swing slowed down, he jumped to the ground. "Here, Peanut."

His four-legged pal roused from his place under the wooden picnic table when Gabe threw Peanut's ball. Rachel settled onto the table bench under the large pecan tree. The shade still felt good on this October afternoon.

Watching Gabe and Peanut romp through the backyard filled her soul with a contentment she hadn't experienced in so long. A squirrel scampered up the tree trunk. A mockingbird chirped from a nearby branch. She'd definitely take life at a slower pace if she went back to Dallas.

If *she went back?* The unexpected kisses she'd shared with Mac yesterday had meant more to her than she'd care to admit. Her vow to never fall in love with her boss again was close to shattering in more pieces than a glass bowl dropped on a tile floor. As Granna kept insisting, God had a great sense of humor. Now she was praying about a possible life that couldn't be more different than the one she'd built for herself in Dallas. A life she'd never have thought to reconsider.

She checked her watch. "Gabe, time to go in and pick which toys you want to take to my place."

"And my clean apron? I can help you with your new 'speriment."

"Sure. I can't try a new gingerbread recipe without help from the best assistant in the world."

The broad grin he flashed her direction warmed her heart. She followed Gabe and Peanut inside. Mac had said she'd have to supervise Gabe's toy choices or he'd try to bring half of what he owned.

Half an hour later, Gabe's backpack was stuffed full. "Can you carry Candy Land for me? We'll play that with Daddy after supper."

"Not tonight, honey. Your dad's working late since Tim is sick and couldn't help him today. He said we won't eat till seven, maybe a little later, so he can finish cleaning the barn."

"Oh."

She tousled his blond hair. "Maybe another night, okay?"

"Okay." He struggled with the zipper before handing the backpack to Rachel for her to zip it up.

By six o'clock, her little assistant had tired of helping in the kitchen and taken his truck, plastic cowboys and horses to the dining room. She could get use to listening to a little boy chatter nearby while making up adventures.

She put the cookie sheet of gingerbread in the oven. It should be done a few minutes before Mac came in to eat. A fruit salad chilled in the refrigerator. The chicken breasts were baking in the top oven. She'd finish the mashed potatoes and set them in the warming oven. That way everything would be ready for Mac when he was done with work.

Out of habit, she flipped the outside lights on about six thirty. Mac would laugh at her for turning on lights a half hour before sunset, but the coyotes sometimes started howling before dark.

"Miss Rachel, Peanut wants to go out," Gabe called to her from the dining room.

"He just went out an hour or so ago. He can wait a few minutes till the gingerbread is done and I can come with you."

"How many minutes?"

"About fifteen. He'll be fine."

She turned on the hand mixer to finish the potatoes. The timer went off for the gingerbread just as she covered the bowl of mashed potatoes with foil.

"Gabe, want to taste our gingerbread while it's warm?"

No answer. That was strange. Surely he hadn't fallen asleep. She went to the dining room. The boy and his dog were gone. *Dear God, no.* That was the only prayer she could manage as she ran out the door. Gabe knew he couldn't play outside alone this time of day. Especially not here, closer to where the coyotes sometimes were.

"Gabe, where are you?" Still no reply. Her pulse

pounded in her ears as she called his name again. There was no sign of which direction they'd gone.

Peanut barked furiously.

"Go away!" Gabe screamed.

Chills traveled up and down every inch of her body as she ran to the south, toward where she'd heard Gabe's voice. When she found them, three coyotes, silhouetted by the mesquite trees, stood about twenty feet away, eyeing the boy and his barking dog.

"Get out of here! Ha! Ha!" She waved her arms and yelled, then threw the biggest rock she could lift at one of them.

The animals trotted off through the grass toward the creek. She knelt and hugged Gabe.

"You're hurting me, Miss Rachel."

"Sweet boy, what were you thinking?"

"What's going on?" Mac ran up to them before Gabe could answer Rachel's question. "I heard Gabe while I was walking toward the kitchen."

She released Gabe. Still trembling, she rose to talk to Mac.

Mac stared at her while he caught his breath.

"Gabe didn't wait for me to go outside with him. But I'm not sure how he got this far." She'd never been so rattled in her life.

"You don't know how he got here?" The hard set of his jaw made her skin prickle. He had a right to be upset, but why was he glaring at her?

"Miss Rachel said wait for her, but Peanut wanted out real bad. He saw a bunny and runned off real fast."

"And you chased him down here?" The obvious answer to her question wouldn't make Rachel's heartbeat slow, but it might help Mac understand what had happened.

"Yes, ma'am. I forgotted about the coyotes."

"Coyotes?" Mac's blazing eyes looked almost ready to catch fire.

"Yes, sir. But Miss Rachel scared them all away."

"That's good. Let's go home now." His terse tone signaled she wasn't misinterpreting the looks he was giving her.

"Miss Rachel has lots and lots fixed for supper, Dad. I helped lots." Gabe reached for his dad's hand and tugged him toward the guest ranch.

Mac shook his head. "We're going home."

"Home?" She looked up at Mac.

"Home. Where someone will watch a child the way they should." He gripped his son's hand.

"That's not fair." Somehow he'd decided all this was her fault.

"Really? You're the one who didn't know how he got out here." The fire in his eyes had turned to a cold glare that chilled her soul.

"There's a good reason for that."

She'd go into more detail about how Gabe must have slipped out while the noise of the hand mixer had kept her from hearing him leave. But not with Gabe standing next to his dad. Not when any discussion with him might become more tense than a little boy should hear.

"Doesn't look like that to me. He's five. You're not." Mac turned his son toward the main house. "Let's go."

Tears stinging her eyes, she stared at their backs until

she could no longer hear Gabe's protests. Mac blamed her for what had happened. The whole incident did look bad, but there was a good explanation.

Surely a man who didn't mind his son wandering on imaginary journeys while watching for snakes and scorpions would listen to what really happened. In the meantime, she had a lot of food to put away. Even more things to sort out.

What had been a kitchen filled with tempting aromas smelled stale enough to almost sour her stomach as she walked inside. No use trying to eat the potatoes or chicken. She should eat something, but even her favorite fruit salad tasted like dirt to her.

Her mind kept replaying the moment when she couldn't find Gabe. She could clearly see the coyotes in the brush. Picture Mac's stony glare as he all but dragged Gabe away. Leaning against the cabinets, she surveyed the spotless kitchen. Wiped down countertops, even the mopped tile floor. Nothing looked the way she'd envisioned it would two hours ago when she took the gingerbread out of the oven.

Swallowing hard, she grabbed her phone from the countertop. Gabe should be in bed by now. Maybe Mac would talk to her. She sent a text. Can we talk?

Her phone chimed, signaling his reply a few minutes later. Can you come by the house?

After letting him know she'd stop by, she went to her room for the LED lantern Mac had given her. Walking would delay what she feared would be a very uncomfortable conversation. Hopefully since he wanted to talk, he'd had time to calm down, or Gabe had told him what had really happened.

Mac greeted her from the back porch. "I was watching for your car."

"No use driving such a short distance." Since he was watching for her, maybe that was good?

"Mind if we talk outside so we don't wake Gabe up?"

"Sure."

Wordlessly, she followed him over to the picnic table. The table they'd sat at when she'd asked him to taste her new barbecue sauce recipes. She turned off the lantern and set it on the table. The tension in the air made her too uncomfortable to sit. So she turned to face him instead.

The shadows from the tree made it hard to see his face well even with the floodlights. But his curt tone of voice didn't sound welcoming.

"Did Gabe tell you what happened?"

"He said he was going to stay in the yard and wait for you."

"Except I told him Peanut could wait fifteen more minutes until the gingerbread finished baking."

"So you're saying he didn't wait for you?"

"Exactly." She placed her hand on his sleeve, but he jerked his arm away. "I finished the mashed potatoes while I waited for the gingerbread, assuming he'd stay in the dining room and play the way he knew he's supposed to do."

"How could you not hear him and a dog go outside? He never does anything quietly."

"The hand mixer I was using to whip the potatoes must have blocked out whatever noise he made."

"You don't need a mixer to block out anything. I know how hard you concentrate when you're fixing food."

"That's not fair. Mixers make more noise than you think. Please listen to me."

"I heard you. But I *saw* my son, who got halfway down to Longhorn Creek alone before you found him. With coyotes menacing him only feet away."

"Gabe deliberately did what he knew he wasn't supposed to do when he went outside alone."

"You put the only son I'll ever have in danger." His voice cracked. Then he spun on his heel and marched toward the back door.

Too stunned to reply, Rachel let him go.

Chapter Thirteen

Wind combined with a pounding rain rattled Mac's bedroom window Thursday morning. Texas was one of those places where a man could get woken up by a thunderstorm. He checked the clock on his nightstand. Almost six. The alarm would go off soon. Might as well get up.

He yawned as he sat on the side of his bed. Another night of not sleeping well. Rachel had texted him Tuesday morning to tell him she'd stay through this weekend, since she knew he couldn't find anyone quickly enough to replace her by Friday. She'd bought groceries yesterday afternoon. He knew, because she'd texted to let him know just before she left for Sunrise.

Aunt Sharon had come back from Fort Worth later than she'd planned, after Gabe was in bed, so he couldn't tell her he hadn't seen Rachel since Monday. One of the few good things happening lately. What wasn't good was that the doctor wanted Mom to have two or three more weeks of rehab. His parents would barely be home in time for Thanksgiving at this rate.

Which meant he'd have to find someone willing to help him out. He couldn't imagine Rachel staying past this Sunday. They hadn't said a word to each other since Monday night. Maybe he and Aunt Sharon could manage without her?

He groaned. And maybe he'd be the next champion professional bull rider while winning the NASCAR championship at the same time. Aunt Sharon was already doing more than her fair share, taking his place with Tim or tending to guests alone every other Sunday.

The wind rattled the window again. Today might be the perfect day to go to town and buy the new work boots he'd been too busy to see about. Tim had called yesterday to say he was feeling better and could work today. But Mac wouldn't think of him working in weather like this and getting sick again. He'd call him in a few minutes.

Then he'd figure out a way to keep Gabe and Aunt Sharon from coming to town with him. He needed to be alone. Gabe would tell Aunt Sharon all about what happened Monday night, but he'd deal with that later. She'd see things his way as soon as he explained how careless Rachel had been with Gabe.

After calling Tim, he shuffled down the stairs, still in his T-shirt and sleep pants. He had coffee going by the time Aunt Sharon walked into the kitchen. Some things were still the same. He couldn't remember how long she'd worn the same red robe, but his dad still teased her about it.

"Are you okay?"

She halted to stare at him as he filled his cup. He

hardly ever beat her to the kitchen, so no wonder she asked how he was doing.

"The rain woke me up." He filled a second mug, then handed it to her.

"Me, too." She blew on the hot coffee. "Good thing Gabe is such a sound sleeper."

"Yeah. I called Tim and told him to stay home. Think I'll go to Tucker's and look for the work boots I need."

"You might as well. None of us will get anything done outside today."

"I'd rather not have company when I go to Sunrise." He studied the mug in his hand.

Her eyebrows arched. "Anything you want to talk about?"

No. He bit back that reply. "I haven't had a day alone since Mom got hurt. I can't go fishing today, so buying boots sounds like a decent substitute."

There was no use wondering if his forced smile looked natural. It couldn't. He'd felt terrible the last several days, no matter how sure he was he'd made the right decision to cut ties with Rachel.

"Okay…" She sipped her coffee. "Maybe if I tell Gabe we'll bake cookies for Rachel, he'll be all right with staying home?"

"Probably."

He'd wait until after he got home to tell her Rachel wouldn't want cookies from any Greer and why.

She grinned. "I think so, too. Rachel deserves a treat she doesn't have to make herself."

"Yes, ma'am."

"You can come with us and ask her to stay two more weeks."

"I doubt she'll do that, especially if I ask."

"Why not?"

"She's been planning to go back to Dallas since the day she came to Sunrise."

Dodging the truth about why he didn't intend to talk to Rachel would buy him the time to enjoy his trip to town. To have a partially pleasant day before he had to relive Monday and explain everything to his aunt. To deal with her shock that Rachel could so neglect Gabe.

Her expression sobered. "Rachel's braved snakes, scorpions and coyotes that scare her to no end so she can do whatever we've asked. But you're too scared to go over to ask her to stay longer? Not every woman is Alicia, honey."

He gulped his too-hot coffee instead of sipping it. His scalded tongue didn't hurt near as much as his heart. He'd trusted Rachel with the one he treasured the most. She'd let him down. "Don't go there. Please." He added the last word only because he was speaking to the aunt he'd idolized all his life.

"All right, honey. What do you want for breakfast?"

He shrugged. "Eggs and bacon."

The rain still hadn't let up as Mac drove into Sunrise. No matter. His mood matched the gray skies better than sunshine. He parked his truck in front of Tucker's. Only a few people were out. Good. The fewer people he had to talk to, the better.

Mandy, the store clerk, greeted him as soon as he

stepped in the store. "Hey, Mac. What can I help you with?"

"I'm looking for work boots. I know my way around. I'll let you know if I need anything." He tried hard to sound cheerful.

"Sure. I'll be happy to get anything from the back when you know what you want."

"Thanks."

He wandered over to the other side of the store. A nice pair of women's boots sat on a too-prominent display. They looked to be just the right size for Rachel. He marched toward the men's section.

"See something you'd like to try on?" Les Tucker, the owner, came up behind him.

Mac jumped. "Maybe." He pointed toward a sturdy brown pair of boots. "I don't see my size here."

"What size? We've got plenty in back."

"Ten."

Les looked all around them, then toward the other part of the store, where only a couple of other customers were. He edged closer to Mac. "Got a minute?" He lowered his voice as he ducked his head.

Not really. But he'd make time to listen if his old friend had a problem he needed to talk about. "Sure. Something wrong?" Mac kept his voice low.

"Word is that your mom might not rush her rehab since Rachel is working out so well. Is that right?"

"Who told you that?" Someone was spreading rumors, since Aunt Sharon had just told him about Mom last night, but he'd keep that to himself until he found out who was saying what.

"Maybe I'd better not say, since you look too shocked for it to be true."

"I found out last night Mom will barely be home in time for Thanksgiving. Aunt Sharon is the only other person who knows that."

Les shook his head. "Good old Sunrise and the rumor mill."

"Yeah." His friend's sarcastic tone didn't make Mac feel any better. "I'd like to try on those boots." He pointed to a pair to his right.

Les didn't budge. Instead he leaned in again. "We've been friends long enough I thought you should know Rachel could be gone sooner than you might be planning."

"What do you mean?"

His friend shouldn't know more about when Rachel might leave than Mac did. But news—or imagined news—traveled faster in Sunrise than a bolt of lightning. One could do as much damage as the other. Especially to a man whose stubborn heart wouldn't cooperate with his brain and quit wishing things hadn't gone so wrong between them.

"Supposedly Lance is helping her get a dream job in Dallas with one of the best restaurants there."

The news should make him happier than hearing beef prices were going sky-high. But it didn't. Hearing Lance's name connected to Rachel's in any way made him feel as if he'd been knocked down and stomped on by someone wearing spurs. Especially since she allegedly was no more than reluctant friends with the man.

"Thanks for the heads-up. But if she's found something that good, I wouldn't think of asking her to stay longer and risk losing a good job."

"Glad things will still be okay for you."

Mac shrugged, hoping to look as indifferent as possible. His pounding heart was anything but indifferent to Les's update. "If she goes, she goes. It's a free country."

"Yeah, it is. I'll get those boots."

Mac nodded. He hoped Les would take a while to find his size. He needed time to…to keep reminding himself of all the reasons he'd be better off the second Rachel left.

Maybe he should talk to her this afternoon. Alone. She could tell him off the way she had yet to do. Tell him she had a good job and didn't need anything from him. And they'd be done.

The ache in his chest argued that his heart didn't want to let go of her. Ever. Why hadn't she been more careful with Gabe?

Trudging through the rain to get into the house a while later didn't improve his mood.

"Looks like you found what you were looking for." Aunt Sharon eyed the box in Mac's hand as she greeted him coming in the back door.

"Yes, ma'am."

"You timed everything just right. Lunch is ready."

"Thanks. I'll put these in my room and be right back."

When Mac returned to the kitchen, Aunt Sharon had the usual sandwiches and soup on the table. Gabe sat in his chair. "We made lots of cookies for us and Miss Rachel."

"Great," he said half-heartedly, seating himself across from his aunt.

"We're going to take them to her this afternoon." His ear-to-ear grin couldn't contrast more with Mac's gloomy attitude.

"Maybe. If it quits raining."

Aunt Sharon's slight shake of her head signaled she wasn't okay with that—or something. "Let's pray, so we can eat."

She thanked God as usual for the food and His blessings, then asked for His wisdom and guidance. That part wasn't normal. Gabe must have told her about Monday evening. No matter how much Gabe might have exaggerated about the coyotes, she'd be more upset after she heard Mac's version.

As soon as she finished the last bite of her sandwich, Aunt Sharon rose and took her dishes to the sink. "Gabe, why don't you watch a movie after you finish eating?"

"But we need to take cookies to Miss Rachel."

"We can do that later. I need to talk to your dad first."

If she was still thinking of taking anything to Rachel, Gabe must not have told her what really happened.

When Mac returned from setting up Gabe's movie in the living room, Aunt Sharon had already settled back into her chair at the table. He took his usual one across from her.

"Gabe said Rachel chased coyotes away from him and Peanut Monday. He hasn't seen Rachel since then and feels awful. He wants to tell her he's sorry for disobeying her and letting Peanut outside when she told him to wait."

"That's a little boy's version. Rachel got so busy, so involved fixing her precious food that she didn't notice when Gabe went out the dining room door. When I found them, she didn't even know how he got there. Her words, not mine." The fear and anger he'd felt that night surged through him again.

"Gabe's words. He remembers she said exactly fifteen minutes until she could come with him. He knows he was wrong."

How could she say such a thing? Almost as if she might take Rachel's side. "Maybe. What Rachel did was more than wrong. She put Gabe in danger. Since she texted me she's leaving after Sunday, that means she knows it, too."

She gasped. "Have you so much as tried to talk to her? To hear her side of things?" Placing her elbows on the table, she leaned toward him.

"Yes, ma'am. After I tucked Gabe in that night."

"What did she say?"

"Some silly thing about how much noise a hand mixer made when she was fixing mashed potatoes."

Looking straight into his eyes, Aunt Sharon took a deep breath. "Gabe needs the chance to make things right with her. And you two need to work things out."

"No, she should have been more careful. Like I told her, Gabe's the only son I'll ever have."

"That's for sure, the way you're treating Rachel. Talk to her."

"I spoke my piece. She made her excuses. There's nothing more to say."

His aunt shook her head. "Yes, there is. Don't be so

stubborn. Like I keep telling you, that woman scares you to death because you're so afraid to trust anyone again."

"That's not true." It was. More than he cared to admit. His heart wanted to talk to Rachel, straighten things out between them. But his head reminded him how that had gone when he'd tried to talk Alicia into staying.

"If what I'm saying isn't true, prove me wrong. Talk to her."

"All right. And maybe I'll ask her to stay until Mom and Dad come home. Tell her it's business only between us, like I did when I hired her."

"What? You didn't. After the way you look at her? The way she looks at you?"

"I did, and I will. We both know finding someone to help us for the rest of the month is almost impossible." His aunt's imagination had been working overtime for too long, but he didn't want to talk about that now. "When she turns me down, you'll finally believe what I said about Monday is true."

"What I believe is true, you don't want to hear." She rose and walked toward the dishwasher. Then turned back toward him. "I don't usually interfere between you and Gabe. But he and I'll take cookies to Rachel after his movie is over. He's miserable and won't feel better until he apologizes to her."

"Fine. Take him over there. I don't mind."

"You're welcome to come, too. Make yourself feel better the way your son wants to do."

Chapter Fourteen

Rachel looked out the large dining room window. For at least the second or third time. Still raining. The dining room was spotless. She'd set out the place mats with boot appliqués on a fall leaf print plus the vases she'd found. Next she'd reorganize her spices?

Not *her* spices. Nothing here was hers. Or would ever be hers. Not after Mac refused to listen to her.

Just as she'd done Monday night, she wouldn't allow herself to think about what might have been. No matter how much she'd tried to deny it, she'd fallen in love with Mac. But if he loved her, he'd have listened to her explanation of how Gabe had gone outside without her realizing it.

She sighed. The rain made bigger puddles on the ground while she wished she could go outside. She'd gotten used to walking, enjoying the trees, birds and squirrels. Watching breathtaking sunsets. Soaking in the welcoming kind of solitude Still Waters Ranch offered. In spite of snakes, coyotes and poison ivy, she'd learned to love this place.

Too bad she'd let her guard down with Mac. He'd turned out to be more dangerous than the creatures she feared.

He'd broken her heart.

That was her fault. Again. He'd never so much as hinted at wanting more than friendship. Until he'd kissed her. If only she hadn't kissed him back…

She trudged into the immaculate kitchen. Rearranging the pantry would help her think less. Caroline Greer's pantry. Not Rachel's, the way it had come to feel lately.

Three more days, and she'd be gone. She blinked away the burning tears trying to slip down her cheeks. Her aching heart had urged her to leave town Monday night. But she had nowhere to go. Nowhere she wanted to go.

Her parents would take her in. Granna would let her sleep on her couch. But then she'd have to explain everything. Telling so many people how she'd made another huge mistake with a man was not what she wanted to do.

A shaft of sunlight streamed through the window over the sink before she finished going through the pantry. The phone in her pocket dinged, signaling an incoming text. Sharon and Gabe wanted to bring cookies over, since the rain had stopped. Gabe wanted to apologize for Monday.

Her throat tightened. Such a sweet little boy. At least she could make things right with one Greer. Plus she could tell him goodbye. How she'd do that, she wasn't sure. But she wouldn't think of hurting him and not letting him apologize if he felt he needed to. She sent the reply. Come on over!

Since Sharon was coming also, she must not be too upset with Rachel, if she was willing to bring Gabe over. She had to know why Gabe wanted to say he was sorry. Surely Mac had told her his version of what happened Monday, and that Sunday was her last day here. So why did she and Gabe want to bring her homemade cookies?

Whatever the reason, Rachel had no intention of telling Sharon or anyone else that she had allowed herself to dream of a life here with Mac. No one would ever know about her one and only horseback ride or Mac's sweet kisses. She doubted he wanted anyone to know what had happened between them.

They knocked on the kitchen door a few minutes later.

"I'm coming." She put on a fake smile before opening the door.

Mac stood behind Sharon and Gabe. That shocked her, and she found herself unable to move, the physical ache she could feel in her chest threatening to overwhelm her. She looked down at Gabe, hoping she could paste on a pretend smile long enough to prevent giving her true feelings away.

"Wipe your feet on the mat before you go in, buddy." Mac's words halted Gabe's steps for a few seconds while he followed his dad's instructions.

"I helped make all kinds of cookies, Miss Rachel. Molasses and sugar cookies." Gabe held out a plastic container to her as he stepped inside.

"Thank you." She took his offered gift as Sharon and Mac followed close behind him. "Y'all must have been busy."

Gabe nodded. "And I wore my apron."

"Good for you." She set the cookies on the island countertop. "There's milk in the fridge if you want to help me eat some of these."

"Can I?" He looked to his dad.

"Just one. I have a feeling you tasted several this morning while you helped make them." Mac lifted his son onto the wooden stool next to the island.

Rachel turned her back to Mac as she grabbed the milk from the fridge. "Anybody else want some?" She paused in front of the cabinet holding the glasses and plates.

Mac shook his head. "No. I'm good."

"No, thanks. I've had more than I should already." Sharon's sober expression made Rachel wonder why she'd come.

She poured milk for herself and Gabe before taking the lid off the cookie container. "Which one should I try first?"

"Both."

"Both?" She leaned against the countertop close to his stool, as if they were the only ones in the room.

He grinned. "Uh-huh. I like both."

So nice to concentrate on a little boy and pretend Mac wasn't here. She took one of each kind of cookie so she could take a bite of both. "Mmm. I like both, too."

Gabe giggled. Sharon's eyes took on a tender look as she watched the exchange between Rachel and Gabe.

Mac's serious expression and stiff posture made her wonder why he'd come. She shouldn't be watching him at all, but her heart wouldn't stop her from glancing at him.

"Miss Rachel, can I tell you something?" Gabe set his half-eaten cookie on his plate.

"Of course you can." She focused on him again.

"I'm sorry I didn't listen when you said to wait till the gingerbread was done." His lip trembled.

"It's okay. We all do things we shouldn't." She patted his arm.

"You're not mad at me?"

"No."

Sliding off the stool, he wrapped his arms around her waist the instant his feet touched the floor. "I'm so glad you're not mad at me."

How she wanted to scoop him up in her arms and hug him back. But he wasn't hers. Never would be. She closed her eyes as he hugged her tighter. If she tried to say anything, her voice might not cooperate with her.

"Can we talk in the dining room after you finish your cookies?" Mac looked over Gabe's head toward her. His stony expression signaled he didn't want Gabe hugging her, much less being near her.

"Okay." But nothing was okay, since Mac looked as if he'd come to finish tearing apart the pieces of her heart he'd missed on Monday night.

Gabe released her. She set him back on his stool. Then took her time as if savoring every last bite of the cookies she could no longer taste. Her foolish emotions wouldn't quit hoping she and Mac could find a way to make things right between them.

"Gabe, I need your help to go check the guest cabins," Sharon said.

"But I haven't seen Miss Rachel in forever."

"She and your daddy need to talk."

"In here or the dining room?" Rachel waited until Gabe and Sharon were gone to speak to the man still standing silently only two feet away.

Mac swallowed hard as he looked into her eyes. "In here is fine. I doubt I'll be here long."

Her thoughts exactly, since he didn't sound or look as if he was here to set things right.

"Mom needs to stay in Fort Worth another two or three weeks till just before Thanksgiving. Can you stay on the ranch longer?"

"You haven't spoken to me in days and now you want me here? Here, where you'll have to see me? Pretend you at least like me?"

He flinched as if she'd slapped him. "We started out business only. Can we possibly go back to that?"

No. Her dry throat wouldn't allow her to get the word out. Her heart wasn't cooperating, either.

But hope or no hope for her and Mac, she didn't want to go back to family right now. Granna wouldn't believe her if she told her there had never been anything between her and Mac. She'd probably already told everyone else in the family about him. Explaining how Rachel had misjudged another man was too painful to think about. Much less talk about over and over again by the time she talked to Granna and her parents.

"I'll stay." For once, her common sense kicked in. If only she'd listened to her head sooner instead of her heart when it came to Mac.

"Really? Instead of heading back to Dallas?"

"Dallas can wait a little while longer for me."

"Thanks." He headed toward the door without tipping his hat.

They'd agreed to go back to business only between them. Business only it would be.

The weekend went by in a blur. Rachel kept as busy as possible. Mac took Gabe with him on the trail ride with the guests and let him help with the roping demonstration, leaving the little boy with Rachel as infrequently as possible. Anyone watching them together on Sunday couldn't possibly suggest Mac should marry her. They spoke to each other only when necessary. She let Mac stay in the dining room with the guests while they ate lunch, pretending she had something to do in the kitchen.

Sun streamed through the curtains of Rachel's bedroom window Wednesday morning. Her *temporary* bedroom. She parted the curtains to watch the squirrels play in the nearby pecan tree. So much for wishing this place might hold the hope of the forever home she longed to find. Her lack of judgment had betrayed her again.

She took her time eating breakfast. Her only chore for the day was buying groceries for the guest ranch. She should email a friend or two in Dallas to tell them she'd be back soon and needed work. The sooner she found another job, the sooner she could find her own place again and the less time she'd be staying with her parents.

But for the first time in her life, thinking about going back to Dallas didn't thrill her. She'd found the quiet solitude and peace she craved at Still Waters Ranch. Until she'd risked falling in love with Mac.

She parked her Mustang in front of Granna's house around eleven. She'd miss seeing her grandmother so often. Miss their lunches together. Where she'd go next, only God knew. But she'd look for another job as a chef. She had excellent references and online reviews now.

And memories. Sweet memories of Gabe and the beautifully rugged land she'd come to love. Bittersweet memories of Mac, of what wasn't meant to be.

As she shut her car door, she shut off her wishful thinking. She'd have to remember to lock her car again when she moved back to Dallas. She'd also have to lock away thoughts of Mac and remember only Gabe.

Granna opened the door as Rachel reached the front porch. "Hi, sugar."

"Hi." Rachel walked into her grandmother's hug. "Ready to go to lunch?"

"Not today. I got hungry for homemade chicken and dumplings, so I made some." Granna grinned as she stepped back and let Rachel into the house.

"I've always loved that."

"I remember." Granna stepped inside. "Karen's having lunch with a friend, so we get time for just us."

"That's great."

Rachel kept an eye on her grandmother as she followed her toward the kitchen. Granna looked and sounded fine. Her steps seemed as spry as ever. But turning down a chance to get out of the house wasn't like her.

"The house smells wonderful." She breathed in the aromas that brought back special times of eating with Granna and Gramps.

She couldn't resist inhaling again after they were seated at the table across from each other. Granna said a short prayer of thanks for their meal. Her eyes sparkled as she took her first bite.

"You must have people coming this weekend, since you're here in town to grocery shop today."

"All the cabins are booked up the next three weekends." Rachel savored another bite of chicken and dumplings.

"Oh." Granna laid her spoon next to her bowl and looked straight at Rachel. "Something isn't making sense here. We need to talk."

"We do?" Rachel set her tea glass on the table.

"Karen's friend Willa told her you'd accepted a job in Dallas with a premier restaurant and would be leaving soon. So, of course, Karen told me."

Rachel shook her head. "I have no idea where I'll work next. I'll look for a job in Dallas first."

"Good. I feel much better, sugar." Granna grinned.

"You do?"

"I didn't say a word to Karen about it, but I was hurt to hear from her you had a new job before you told me."

"I'd never do that." Her delicious meal had lost its taste. "Why would anyone think I have a job lined up in Dallas?"

"Willa cleans Lance's house, you know."

Granna took another bite of dumplings, looking as content as could be and in no hurry to finish telling the story she'd started. Rachel fought to keep from drumming her fingers on the table.

"Karen says Willa is sure since her friends who work at the Morning Glory think Lance likes you. But he's too shy to say anything. So Willa started kidding Lance about it. Lance says there is nothing between the two of you. But he all but told Willa you'd be going back to Dallas soon."

"I'll talk to him before I go to the grocery store." So much for the pleasant afternoon she'd planned. The man she'd thought was a harmless fan wasn't so harmless. The sarcastic remark Mac had made last week about her going back to Dallas made a little more sense now. He had heard the rumors, too.

If only everything else he'd said or done the last week or so made sense. But it didn't. He'd made up his mind about what he thought about her. She'd be better off forgetting him no matter how much her heart wasn't cooperating with her mind.

"You set Lance straight. He has no right spreading false stories about you." Granna pointed her spoon in Rachel's direction, as if to emphasize her point.

"I'll do that." She had a hard time concentrating during the rest of the meal. She barely tasted her dumplings, one of her favorites, which Granna had made for her since she was little. The more she puzzled over Granna's news, the more exasperated she got.

A few minutes after one o'clock, Rachel hugged Granna goodbye. "Please tell Karen the truth about me."

"I will. I'll tell her and anyone else I hear talking about you."

"Thanks. I love you."

"Love you, too, sugar." Granna kissed Rachel's cheek.

Rachel drove straight to the café. Someone backed their car out of a space a few feet from the door. She took it.

"Good to see you." The hostess offered her greeting the instant Rachel stepped inside. "Is your grandmother meeting you here?"

"No. I need to talk to Lance."

"I think he's in his office." Misty finished wiping off a menu. Then she pointed toward the back. "The stairs are at the back of the kitchen, but—"

"Thanks." Rachel turned to walk toward the kitchen.

"But you can't just walk in there."

"Today I can." Rachel dodged the woman as she tried to stop her.

Customers came in, leaving the flustered hostess no choice but to seat them and let Rachel continue on her way. The small second-floor area looked like a huge storage room, filled with extra chairs, linens and other supplies stacked all around. She peeked into a room with an open door. Lance sat at his desk staring at a computer screen. She knocked on the door frame as she stepped into the room.

"Rachel? Hi! Come on in. Can I help you?" He rose.

"I hope so. My grandmother told me people are talking about my new dream job in Dallas and how I'll be leaving soon."

"Congratulations. When do you start?" He extended his hand to her.

"I hate to be rude, but I heard you already know all that." She stepped back.

His eyes widened. "No more than we've talked about, how would I?"

Was this man she barely knew telling her the truth? Logic seemed to agree with him. "The lady who cleans your house is absolutely sure you know I've found some kind of wonderful job in a premier restaurant in Dallas."

"Ohhh. I think I understand now." He smiled.

Nothing he'd said made her feel like smiling.

"Willa wouldn't tell me who, but someone is sure I've got a crush on you. I told her that would be a waste of time, since you'd surely be going back to Dallas soon as a premier chef."

"Really?"

"I'm sorry, but I had no idea she'd take me so seriously." He shrugged. "The joys of living in a small town, I guess."

"I guess so." He appeared to be truthful and sincere. "Sorry I barged in on you like this."

"It's okay. I don't blame you."

"Thanks. I'll let you get back to work." She walked out of the office.

The way rumors sprouted and grew in Sunrise, there was no telling what people might be speculating about concerning her and Mac. But they'd soon be proven wrong about that, too.

Chapter Fifteen

Rachel sipped her morning coffee while sitting in a rocking chair on the porch of the cabin closest to the dining room. Snuggling into her hoodie felt good after last night's cold front had dropped the temperature to the upper forties this morning. Perfect weather for keeping her fall tradition of making pumpkin pies from scratch. For staying too busy to think.

Gabe had been talking for a week about all the candy he'd collect at the Fall Festival at church tomorrow night, so he'd probably enjoy a real jack-o'-lantern. Maybe she'd make one for him.

Sharon would be bringing him over soon so she could clean the guest cabins. With Mac out in some pasture where he couldn't object, Sharon still brought the boy to stay with her. The two of them would have a fun morning together.

A morning with so much to do that she could turn down Sharon's usual invitation for lunch when she came to pick up Gabe. Any excuse to keep from spending a few minutes with Mac was great. Sharon must still have hopes the two of them could patch things up. Rachel didn't. Not as long as she could keep her heart from overruling her mind.

A light tapping sounded on the back door not long after Rachel set two nice-size pie pumpkins on the countertop of the kitchen island. Gabe's little knock. "Come in."

He marched in with his aunt. "Want to go 'sploring? Snakes don't like the cold."

Rachel laughed. Even Gabe was sympathetic about her fears. "Not today. Let's make jack-o'-lanterns instead."

"Really?"

"Get your jacket off first." Sharon snagged him before he could trot over to Rachel.

"Really. I'm going to make pumpkin pies this afternoon. I'll let you help get everything ready."

"I don't remember ever eating a pie made from fresh pumpkins," Sharon said as she stood beside Gabe.

"They're worth all the work. It's easy to taste the difference from the canned filling." Rachel pulled Gabe's blue apron from the drawer by the sink. "You'll need this. Making jack-o'-lanterns is messy."

He grinned as she slipped the apron loop over his head. "We'll make the bestest jack-o'-lantern ever."

"We sure will."

Gabe wasn't the best helper to have around while she scooped out the pumpkins. But he was the best company she could ask for. As long as she didn't pay too close attention to his warm brown eyes that looked so much like his father's.

"You can help me rinse the seeds. Then we'll toast them."

"You make toast out of seeds?" He stared wide-eyed as she put the seeds in the colander.

She smiled at him. "Not toasted bread. We'll rinse them good, then put them in the oven for a few minutes. They're delicious with some cinnamon sprinkled on them."

"Sugar, too? I like cinnamon-sugar toast." He licked his lips.

"I'll add sugar just for you."

Rachel finished carving a simple jack-o'-lantern not long before Sharon came to get her helper.

"Look, Aunt Sharon." Gabe pointed to the pumpkin sitting on the countertop the second his aunt walked in.

"That's very nice. Ready for lunch?" Sharon's gaze included Rachel.

"Yes, ma'am. Miss Rachel says I can take my jack-o'-lantern home. And seed toast, too."

"Seed toast?" Sharon looked to Rachel.

"Toasted pumpkin seeds." She handed a plastic container to Sharon.

"You've more than earned letting me fix your lunch today."

"Thanks, but I want to make the pies this afternoon. I won't have time tomorrow before the guests come."

"You're amazing."

"Thank you."

She swallowed the lump in her throat as Sharon ushered Gabe outside. The one Greer she wanted to hear say those words wasn't speaking to her. Granted, she wasn't speaking to him, either.

The usual Friday routine kept Rachel too busy to eat lunch at the Greer house, too. Or so she texted Sharon when the sweet woman invited her to lunch. In spite of Sharon's constant matchmaking, Rachel had come to love and appreciate such a kind person. Another Greer she'd miss.

By five o'clock, Rachel had the food and dining room ready for the guests who should be coming in any time. Readying herself was not as easy. She looked the part of ranch chef in her jeans and peach-colored long-sleeve shirt with shiny pearl snaps. But her heart wasn't ready to see Mac whenever he brought the guests in.

Maybe she shouldn't have agreed to stay longer. Dodging Mac tomorrow wouldn't be hard to do. Seeing him in church on Sunday would be rough. Even rougher on her heart. She'd have been better off letting people think she'd found a new job so she could have left.

Allowing people to believe a lie wasn't right. She squared her shoulders. She'd face the heartache she'd once again brought on herself. Deal with it just as she'd faced her fear of snakes and coyotes. She'd keep her word and stay. Two weeks more than planned. But no more. No matter if Mac's mother had to remain in Fort Worth longer.

Mac soon opened the door for the guests to come in.

"This place smells wonderful." A blonde woman inhaled deeply as she walked inside.

"We've got the best chef in Texas." Mac's thin smile didn't reach his eyes as he followed the couples inside.

The quick glance he gave her made her heart feel as if he'd sliced it with the knife she'd just used to cut the corn bread.

"Rachel will feed you well. I'll see y'all in the morning." He left before anyone could pick up a plate for Rachel to serve them.

On Saturday morning, Mac brought Gabe over as she finished clearing breakfast dishes off the last table. Taking his son on the trail ride must not have worked well.

"Hi, Miss Rachel." Gabe trotted in, brown teddy bear in hand.

"Hi to you." The smile she gave him was one of the few genuine ones she'd managed all week.

"Thanks for the pumpkin yesterday." Mac remained close to the door.

"You're welcome." She couldn't keep from staring into his eyes. Brown eyes without the warmth she was used to seeing lately whenever he'd looked at her.

"I need to get going."

Instead of reaching for the knob, he returned her stare. How she wished she could know his thoughts. His tense posture made him seem to be struggling to not look at her as hard as she was trying not to pay any attention to him. After the way he'd blamed her for Gabe disobeying her, she didn't want to know what he was thinking. She had enough to forget without him saying something else she didn't want to hear.

He looked from her to Gabe. "Be good and—"

"And do what Miss Rachel says." Gabe finished the sentence his dad said every Saturday.

"Right." He went out the door as quickly as he'd done last night. Again without tipping his hat to her.

She spent a pleasant, busy morning with Gabe the way she'd been doing the last several weeks. He helped her finish cleaning the kitchen, and they took a short walk outside, then came in to start getting ready for the noon meal.

But Gabe didn't chatter about anything and everything the way he usually did. He said so little while they cleaned up after lunch that she was tempted to touch his forehead to see if he had a fever. While she loaded the dishwasher, he and his teddy bear crawled up onto the stool by the island.

She kept an eye on her little assistant while she put meat and cheese in the fridge for whenever Mac came in to grab a sandwich. *If* he came in. The way he'd acted the last few days, he might fix his own lunch at his house. The sooner her stubborn heart accepted such a possibility, the better off she'd be.

"Know what, Miss Rachel?" Gabe hugged his bear close.

"What?" She walked over to him. His face wasn't flushed. He hadn't coughed all day.

"I miss Monnie and Granddaddy a lot." His listless tone tore at her heart.

She smiled, wishing she could do something to help him feel better. "I'm sure you do."

"When are they coming home? I forgot." His innocent eyes searched her face as he waited for her answer.

"Your dad says about two weeks or so." She leaned in closer to him.

"And then you leave?"

She swallowed the lump in her throat. "That's the plan."

"I don't like that plan. I want Monnie and Granddaddy home real bad." He buried his face in his bear's fur. "But then I'll miss you."

And she'd miss him. She patted his arm. "It's okay, little guy. I'll be back to visit my grandmother. Maybe I could come see you, too."

"You promise?"

The stinging tears in her eyes made it impossible not to nod her head. "I'll try my best when I come back to Sunrise."

He wrapped his bear-filled hand and free hand around her neck, almost knocking her off balance. "I love that plan. Bunches and bunches."

Me, too. Her heart whispered words she dare not say out loud while she leaned in and held him as tightly as he gripped her.

Mac stepped into the dining room. With the trail ride, done, he'd grab a quick sandwich, then let Gabe help with the horses and keep his son away from Rachel awhile. He froze in the doorway going into the kitchen. *Oh, no.* Rachel was not supposed to be hugging his boy. Gabe wasn't supposed to have his little arms around her neck.

What he saw panicked him. Both of them caring about each other so much they hadn't heard him open the dining room door or step inside. Before either of them could see him, he backed away. He fled outside as quietly as he'd come in.

He ran until he reached the safety of the barn. No one could see him in here. Or hear him gasping for air. He closed his eyes as he leaned against the rough boards. Letting down his guard and falling in love with a woman he knew would leave was bad enough. Being so worried about protecting his own heart that he'd missed seeing his son had also come to love her was so much worse. He'd let Gabe down. His son was already hurting. Before Rachel ever left.

If he didn't need her help so badly, he'd tell her to leave tonight. But he couldn't afford to cancel two weeks of reservations. Cold weather and holidays would soon cut down drastically on the bookings they needed to help keep the ranch going.

The reality of his situation slammed him in his gut. He had no one else to watch Gabe during the day on Saturdays while he took care of guests. His family had to have the money from those people to stay in business, to keep the ranch in the family. Too many small ranchers had already given up the struggle to survive and sold out.

"Lord, please help me." One short, desperate prayer was all he could manage. All he knew to do.

Mac felt like a machine running on fumes as he went through the rest of the day, but he'd thought of one way to cut back on Gabe's Saturday time with Rachel by the time he needed to start the campfire.

He stepped inside the kitchen, where Gabe was helping Rachel clean up from supper. "Hey, buddy. Want to help me make the fire and set up the chairs?"

"Can I?" Gabe's face lit up.

He nodded. "Take your apron off and let's go."

"I'll see you later. Sit by me?" Gabe paused on his way out to look up at Rachel.

"Sure." She patted his head.

Before he and Gabe finished setting everything up, Aunt Sharon joined them. "Need some help?"

"No, thanks. Take a chair. I'm sure you're tired." Mac unfolded one for her.

"Tired but happy. I checked our online reviews a few minutes ago. Nothing but four and five stars. They love our little bed-and-breakfast–style taste of the West. And the food."

"That's great." Mac helped Gabe set up the last chair.

"My favorite is the one from the Reese couple. They said since Rachel's the only worker who isn't family, the best way to keep from losing her is for you to marry her."

"Oh, no," he said out loud, keeping his back to her as he started the fire.

"I think the two of you need to talk, don't you?"

A couple walking toward them ended whatever else his aunt wanted to say. Maybe it was one small way God was answering his prayer for help. He needed more help than he'd thought. His aunt's hints about how he and Rachel should be together were bad enough. Using the Reeses' review to spur her suggestion that they should marry sent chills up and down his spine.

Rachel was the last person to come out to the fire.

Because of that, she missed her chance to sit by Gabe, since Mac had managed to seat his son between himself and Aunt Sharon.

Then his aunt stood and grinned in Rachel's direction. "Take my chair, honey. I want to talk to the lady who quilts and get hints from her." Without waiting for a response, his aunt changed chairs.

Mac was in more trouble than he wanted to think about.

Chapter Sixteen

At breakfast Thursday morning, Mac realized how little he'd seen of Rachel since Sunday. He'd rushed home after church to check on a cow that was due to calve. Or so he'd told Miss Connie when she'd asked him to go to lunch with her and Rachel.

Gabe wandered into the kitchen as Mac finished his last bite of scrambled eggs. He and his teddy bear took the chair closest to Mac.

"You're up early." He grinned at his son, still in his puppy-print pajamas, who looked more asleep than awake.

"Me and Miss Rachel are going 'splorin' while Aunt Sharon cleans cabins."

"What are y'all going to look for this morning?" Sharon grinned from her spot across the table.

Gabe shrugged. "We won't know till we find the ladybug's letter."

Another routine Mac needed to put a stop to as long as it included Rachel. She'd made herself scarce most of the week, but his son's affection for her hadn't dimmed. He talked about her too often. Mentioning exploring with her the first thing after he got up was not a good sign.

"You should stay with Aunt Sharon today. Miss Rachel might be as busy as she was last week and be too nice to tell you."

The puzzled look in Gabe's eyes signaled Mac's feeble reasoning hadn't made sense. "But I'm her best 'sistant when she's busy."

"You should be Aunt Sharon's assistant today."

The slight shake of his aunt's head said she wasn't buying a word of it. But hopefully today she'd keep her promised not to interfere with decisions he made concerning Gabe. Right now the stormy look in her eyes meant she was probably biting her tongue to keep quiet.

Gabe shook his head. "But I promised Miss Rachel I'd go 'splorin' with her."

"Aunt Sharon's been working extra hard lately. You should help her instead."

"But we always keep promises. You said so."

"Yeah, but I'm sure Miss Rachel will understand why I say you should help your aunt today." Mac rose. "I'll see you at lunch. You can tell me all about how good you are at cleaning cabins."

"Daddy?"

Mac paused on his way to the back door. "What?"

"Why are you mad at me?" Gabe cocked his head the way he usually did when he was thinking deeply. He looked close to tears.

Walking back to his son, he knelt beside his chair. "I'm not mad at you, buddy."

"Uh-huh." His lip quivered.

"No, I'm not." He patted Gabe's arm.

"You wouldn't stay in town and let me have chicken strips Sunday." Tears spilled onto his cheeks. "Now you don't want me to 'splore with Miss Rachel."

Mac swallowed the lump in his tight throat. He was mad. At himself. But he couldn't explain all that to a five-year-old. A little boy who expected his dad to do as he'd told him to do—to keep his word. To keep promises.

"You're right, buddy. Keep the promise you made to go explore with Miss Rachel."

A beaming smile dried Gabe's tears as quickly as they'd started. "I will."

"I'll see you at lunch."

The heaviness in Mac's heart made it hard for him to stand. The harder he fought to protect Gabe, the more they both ended up being with Rachel. He had no intention of ever letting his boy know how much it hurt to be abandoned by someone he loved. Accomplishing that was getting harder, and more frustrating, every day.

"I'm praying for you, honey." Aunt Sharon paused to look straight into his eyes before carrying dirty dishes to the sink.

"I could use all the prayers you've got time for." He trudged out the door.

Except she'd pray for the exact opposite of what he'd asked God to do. Protecting his heart, protecting his son from a woman who'd be gone soon was the right thing to do. The best thing. Now all he had to do was convince his stubborn heart to agree.

When Mac came in for lunch, Gabe talked and talked about his adventure with Rachel. No matter how much he tried to turn his son's attention to something else.

That afternoon, he rushed through checking fences in the south pasture. Hurrying Tim was never easy, but he'd managed to do it. He walked into the kitchen a few minutes after four.

Aunt Sharon stood at the counter with the mixer on, stirring something. With her back to him, she didn't realize he'd come in.

"Looks like Gabe talked you into making a cake or something for dessert."

She didn't budge or respond. He raised his voice as he repeated his sentence.

"Something wrong, Mac?" Aunt Sharon turned the mixer off, then whirled to face him.

"No. We finished early. Thought I'd spend a little extra time with Gabe."

"Sure. He's playing in his room."

His aunt's eyes looked full of questions, but she kept quiet and didn't try to stop him from going upstairs.

"Hey, buddy." Mac paused in the doorway of Gabe's room. "Want to go outside and play on the swings?"

"Yes, sir!" Gabe jumped up and ran to hug him.

"I'll go clean up. You put away your toys."

Mac gave his son another push on the swing. He was thankful for perfect weather, a quiet backyard and a little boy who loved to play. He'd have to find ways to do things like this more often. To not rely on others to see to Gabe.

"Me and Miss Rachel had so much fun this morning." Gabe interrupted Mac's dark thoughts.

"I'm sure you did."

"I forgot to tell you we played on the swings, too. She can push me high like you. Just not as long."

Was there a way to stop Gabe from wanting to be with Rachel so much? He'd promised himself his son would never know the pain of being deserted. Thanks to him letting his guard down concerning Rachel, he might have left Gabe open to the very thing he feared. Gabe would miss her terribly if he didn't find a way to sever the boy's ties to Rachel soon.

"Daddy, why don't I have a mama?"

"What?" Mac froze.

"All the kids at church have a mama. Why don't I have one?"

"Well… Because…" He sucked in a ragged breath. "That's a hard question to answer. Can I pray about it and get back to you later?"

"God knows everything. He'll tell you why so you can tell me."

"That's right, buddy. God knows everything."

How could he tell a five-year-old that his mother had deserted him before his second birthday? The very woman who'd named him Gabriel because he looked so angelic with his blond hair and brown eyes. She'd turned her back on both of them. Left them for a life with a director and the chance he offered her for acting jobs in California.

How Mac wished that crew had never chosen Sunrise as the place to film their small-town story. Never given Alicia a role as an extra. Except, she'd already grown so restless it would have only been a matter of time until she left for some other reason.

His gut wrenched as the painful memories seared his heart like a branding iron.

"Keep pushing, Daddy."

That's what he'd do. Keep pushing the swing. Keep pushing through the pain whenever it ambushed him like this. He'd do his best to give Gabe a stable, loving home. So his son would always be secure in knowing he was loved and wanted.

Gabe wouldn't miss having a mother and wouldn't want to know why she wasn't here. And he wouldn't miss Rachel when she left Sunrise.

"Supper's ready." Aunt Sharon stepped out onto the back porch.

"Yippee!" Gabe jumped to the ground. Mac followed him inside.

Mac kept the supper conversation centered on new calves and rumored higher beef prices. Aunt Sharon helped him out by talking about her upcoming plans with Harry on Sunday evening. Maybe things were finally turning around with his world.

He played a couple of video games with Gabe before giving him a bath and getting him ready for bed. Nice way to end what had turned out to be a much better day than he'd thought. He'd tackle a little bookkeeping after Gabe went to bed.

"I'm ready for bed, Daddy." Teddy bear in hand,

Gabe wandered into the living room while Mac and Aunt Sharon watched the news.

He followed his son upstairs. Gabe laid his head on his pillow as Mac knelt beside the twin-size bed. "Ready to pray before you go to sleep?"

"Uh-huh." Gabe closed his eyes. Mac did the same. He thanked God for his fun morning with Miss Rachel, for his time with Daddy. "God, would you give me a mama? I'd really, really like a mama. Amen."

Mac almost choked before he too said, "Amen."

"Aren't you gonna pray?" Gabe's wide eyes signaled his surprise that Mac hadn't added his usual prayer after Gabe's.

"Sure." Mac closed his eyes again. He stumbled through a few words of thanks for his workday.

"Amen." Gabe grinned when Mac opened his eyes again. He wrapped his arms around Mac's neck. "G'night."

"Good night." Mac kissed his son's cheek. "See you in the morning." Mac tucked the airplane quilt and sheet around the little guy's shoulders.

As soon as he trudged downstairs, he went to his office. The busy fall season hadn't left him much time for accounting. Mom and Dad couldn't come home soon enough.

Coffee cup in hand, Aunt Sharon intercepted him in the hall. "We need to talk, Malachi."

"About what?" No one in this family used his full name unless something serious was going on, so whatever she had to say must be important.

"About the past week or so. About you." She started down the hall.

He followed her to the kitchen, her favorite place to talk. She paused by the counter where the coffeepot sat. "Want some?"

"No, thanks."

His coffee-chugging aunt would sleep fine drinking coffee an hour or so before going to bed. He wouldn't. He hoped whatever she was fixing to say wouldn't cost him more sleep than coffee would. She took her usual chair at the small table. Mac seated himself in his spot across from her.

"Let me tell you what really happened when Gabe and Peanut saw those coyotes."

"You can't know what really happened. You've only talked to Gabe."

"Rachel hasn't mentioned that evening. And I haven't asked." She stirred in the cream she'd added. "But Gabe has told me a lot."

"Gabe exaggerates. Like any other kid his age." His aunt knew that, so whatever Gabe had said would be easy to refute.

"Sometimes, yes." Her serious expression signaled he might be in for a rough time. "Gabe said he told you he never intended to leave the yard of the guest ranch without Rachel. Why didn't you listen to him?"

"I did. But Rachel's the adult, who should have seen he was never out there alone regardless."

She sipped her coffee without taking her eyes off him. "Instead of running from coyotes that scare her to no end, she ran toward your son. And scared the coyotes off."

"Which she wouldn't have had to do if she'd been watching Gabe more carefully."

The picture of Aunt Sharon with the mixer running earlier shoved its way into his mind. She hadn't heard a word he'd said. But still, Rachel should have kept a closer eye on a young boy.

"I can't watch Gabe every second. Neither can you. You're being entirely unfair to Rachel." She got up to refill her cup, turning her back on him, her way of deliberately ignoring the way he shook his head at her.

Mac fought the temptation to ditch his manners and respect for his aunt and walk out of the kitchen. Her meddling was stirring up doubts about his conclusions with Rachel.

"Has Rachel said exactly when she's leaving? Right after she finishes lunch that last Sunday or later?" She took her chair again.

Why she'd changed the subject, he didn't know. Maybe she'd realized he was right about Rachel, even if she didn't want to admit it. But just in case she'd decided to go at him from a different angle, he braced himself. "I haven't asked her."

"What if she doesn't really want to leave?"

Now he knew what she really wanted to talk about. One last stab at matchmaking before Rachel left for good. And it *would* be good for him. Especially after he'd learned she had her dream job lined up in Dallas. She couldn't wait to get back to the big city. The sooner she was gone, the sooner the threats to his heart would go with her.

"Did you hear what I asked you? *Really* hear it?" She looked straight into his eyes.

"Yes, ma'am, I did. Yes, Rachel really wants to leave. She's got a job waiting for her in Dallas."

"Oh?" Both her eyebrows quirked up. "When did she tell you that?"

"She didn't."

"Connie hasn't said a word about anything like that. How do you know?" She sipped her coffee.

"Les Tucker told me."

"And Les knows this how?"

Mac shrugged. Nailing down the source of a rumor in Sunrise would be about as easy as trying to catch a fast horse on foot. "He wouldn't say. But Les doesn't lie."

"True. But he could be sincerely wrong."

"Rachel's not cut out for ranch life. She'd have never have come here if the job wasn't temporary."

"She's faced her fears of snakes and scorpions, and she scared off three coyotes. Gabe told me." Her eyes would soon be boring a hole in him if she didn't look away. "She's faced her fears better than you have. Better than you're doing now."

Mac forced himself not to look away from her. He could stand his ground as well as she could.

"So she wasn't cut out for this place at first. But Rachel has changed."

"Working in Dallas is the farthest thing there is from living here."

"Oh, Malachi Owen." Sadness etched her eyes and downturned mouth. "Don't make the same mistake I made so many years ago."

Using his full name twice in a few minutes. Adding in his middle name meant she was deadly serious about something. "I don't understand." But watching her deflate in front of him made him want to understand whatever she felt was so important.

She took a deep breath. "Alicia hurt you like no one else ever has, but—"

"Don't go there. You know better."

He'd never been so curt with his beloved aunt. The whole family knew why Alicia had deserted him and Gabe.

"Yes, I do know better. I let the love of my life get away when I was about your age. Just before my twenty-eighth birthday. The worst birthday of my life. Don't repeat my mistake. Don't push Rachel away forever."

The thick lump in his throat prevented him from replying. The raw pain of what Alicia had done returned any time he spent too long thinking about the past. Rachel was leaving of her own free will. To live the life she wanted, that made her happy and that would have made him miserable. More miserable than he was now.

"Let go of your fear, honey." She leaned closer to him.

"I'm being a realist. Rachel doesn't want what I want."

"She does. She'd stay. Talk to her."

"About what? Not taking her dream job in Dallas? Staying here and being a small-time chef with no chance for anything else?"

"No. About staying here and loving you, because you love her."

His heart pounded faster with every word she spoke. Every true word. He did love Rachel.

"No." He could barely force the word from his tight throat.

"Yes. She loves you. You love her. Anyone who sees the two of you together can tell. Even ranch guests who aren't playing matchmaker like Connie or I have."

Shaking his head was all Mac could manage. He'd made a colossal mess of everything if his feelings were that obvious. His aunt was wrong about Rachel. Yes, she'd kissed him as if she cared as much about him as he did her. But a woman who loved him wouldn't have a job lined up in Dallas, of all places.

Aunt Sharon sucked in another dramatic breath. "As I said, don't repeat my mistakes, honey. I let go of a love I should have never lost. A love I never got back."

As if she wanted this unknown part of her past to sink in, she paused. Then she went on.

"All Franklin had ever wanted was to be a police officer. But a good friend of mine lost her dad in the line of duty, so all I could think about was how dangerous that life would be. I broke off our engagement."

"You did?"

He'd never known his aunt to be afraid of anything. If this was God helping him see the error of his ways, why hadn't He taken away his love for Rachel? Love for another woman who would only leave him. If not for this dream job in Dallas, a different one after she tired of the ranch and him.

"Those teaching positions I took in glamorous places all over the world were my way of running from the pain I'd brought on myself. Coming here this summer for a sabbatical was the best thing I've done in years. God planted me where I truly belong."

She reached across the table and placed her hands over his. "I've been happy to help you so Caroline and Rodger can concentrate on getting her well. And..."

"And what?"

Her drama sucked him in again. The hole she was digging for him got deeper by the minute.

Her eyes sparkled in a way he'd never seen before. "God has allowed me to find love here. Harry and I plan to marry as soon as possible after your parents return."

"Really?"

"Really." An impish grin lit up her face. "If you tell anyone our secret, I'll know exactly who to blame for the gossip. You're the only one I've told."

"I won't say a word." He wouldn't think of betraying her confidence.

She sobered. "Promise me you'll talk to Rachel. Really talk to her. Heart to heart."

"I..."

"Don't you dare say can't. The sooner you propose to her, the better."

He swallowed hard. If she was right about Rachel, he'd be crazy to let her go. But if his aunt was wrong...

"Go for a walk with her tomorrow. A long walk. Tim can finish the ranch work alone for one day."

He shook his head. If he decided to talk to Rachel, he couldn't work up that kind of courage by tomorrow.

"Honey, do it. She's worth the risk."

His turn to take in a long breath. Then another one.

"Rachel will leave only if you let her. It's up to you."
She patted his hand as if he was Gabe's age.

"I'll think and pray about what you've said."

He trudged upstairs to his room. He could let Rachel
go and be miserable. Or he could open his heart to her,
bare his soul and risk worse misery later.

It was an impossible choice.

Chapter Seventeen

Rachel made as many extra trips as possible while clearing lunch dishes off the tables on Saturday. Mac had come to the kitchen asking for a sandwich. Thirty minutes ago. She'd caught him studying her more times than she could count. Never looking away from her whenever she looked his way. He hadn't taken his eyes off her last night when he'd brought the guests in for supper. Her nerves couldn't handle much more.

"I gots all the salt and pepper shakers in the kitchen now."

"Thanks." She tossed Gabe a fake smile.

The little boy followed her around the dining room, eager to do whatever else she asked. She racked her scrambled brain for any subject she could suggest he go talk to his dad about in the kitchen.

But her mind wouldn't cooperate. Her heart longed to sit and talk to Mac. And ask him…what? He'd told her and showed her how he felt after she'd tried to explain why she couldn't have known Gabe would go outside alone.

Mac still sat on the stool at the kitchen island when she came back into the room.

His face lit up the instant he saw her. "You make the best sandwiches ever. See you at the campfire tonight?"

"Uh…okay." She concentrated on the dishpan in her hands instead of him.

He grabbed his hat off the stool beside him as he rose. He tipped it to her before he left. She placed the pan full of dishes on the countertop before she dropped them. Then took several deep breaths, willing her thudding heart to slow down.

After she dawdled cleaning up from supper, she was the last one to the campfire the same as last week. The only empty chair sat between Mac and Gabe. She froze. Sharon didn't budge from her spot next to one of the other women. Rather than make a scene, Rachel took the chair.

She knew nothing about branding, so no one expected her to say anything while Mac demonstrated that by searing a piece of wood with the hot iron. With all eyes on him, no one thought it strange for her to study him, too. He looked so natural, so at home with the firelight flickering on him while he talked about cows.

Her heart wrenched. Her wishful thinking of being at home here with him had betrayed her. Never again. Home would be Dallas or some other large city. The opposite of what she'd thought she might have here.

Too soon, he finished and took his spot next to her. She shivered. Maybe from the breeze that had picked up. Maybe from sitting too close to Mac. The way he'd acted since last night had had her too rattled to think about grabbing something warmer to wear.

Mac stood and took his denim jacket off. "Here. My flannel shirt is heavier than the cotton shirts you like for working in a hot kitchen." He draped his jacket over her shoulders.

"Thank you." Shadows or no evening shadows, she doubted she imagined that everyone around was smiling at the scene Mac created.

The breeze got cooler. The guests didn't linger much longer. Mac started extinguishing the fire.

"Time to get ready for bed." Sharon walked over to Gabe and laid her hand on his shoulder.

"I want to watch for falling stars with Miss Rachel."

Mac looked toward his aunt instead of his son. "Not tonight, buddy. Go with Aunt Sharon."

"Aw, Daddy."

"You can look at stars another night." Sharon ushered the boy toward the main house.

Rachel grabbed her chair to fold. Then picked up another. Before Mac finished putting out the fire, she'd folded every chair. "Um, where should I put your jacket before I go in?"

"I'll get it tomorrow after everyone checks out."

"Okay." Her heart pounded as quickly as she wished she could run. Instead, she put one foot in front of the other, as if everything was as right as the most perfect soufflé she'd ever made.

Which it wasn't.

Since yesterday, Mac had been acting the same way

he had before they'd kissed. A tender shine danced in his eyes when he glanced toward her. He hadn't moved away whenever they'd ended up near each other. But she dared not allow her hopes for a future with him to blossom again.

She wouldn't let him or any other man cloud her judgment anymore.

During lunch the next day, she did her best to keep her distance from him. She fussed over the silk flowers by the coffeepot. She checked to see the tea pitcher was full. Then straightened the napkins stacked next to the silverware.

He did his best to frustrate her every effort. "I saved the last chicken thigh for you, since I've seen you grab that first several times." He took the tongs and set the piece on the last empty plate. Her plate.

He didn't take his place at the little table behind the serving table until she seated herself. And stayed until the last guest had finished eating. While checking everyone out, he seemed to take every chance he could to look across the room at her while she cleaned up. The last guest finally left. Rachel hurried into the kitchen with a half-full dishpan. She'd finish clearing tables after Mac left.

"Need some help?" He followed her into the kitchen.

"No." She busied herself loading the dishwasher with the few plates she'd carried in.

"I'll saddle horses while you finish. Since no one will be back until four or after, want to go for a ride with me again?"

She shook her head. "I...don't think so. No."

"Please. I'd like to straighten out a few things between us before you leave."

"What does that mean?" She grabbed the empty dishpan, not sure if she should stay or leave.

"I'll explain while we ride. Please?"

He was acting the way he used to, but wasn't. The intensity in his gaze the last couple of days, his tone of voice—something had changed. If he confused her any more, her head would be spinning enough to make her dizzy.

"Okay. I'll meet you at the corral when I'm through." Maybe. She would, because her heart wouldn't let her tell him no.

His eyes sparkled. He tipped his hat to her before walking out the back door.

Half an hour later, she headed outside into the sunshine of a perfect early-November day. Comfortable long-sleeve-shirt weather. Except she was anything but comfortable about why she'd agreed to ride with Mac again. Why she couldn't force the words from her tight throat to tell him no and run back inside.

As she halted next to him and the saddled horses, he looked down at her. "I'd like you to have better memories of riding before you take that perfect job you found in Dallas."

Unbelievable—he'd heard the rumors, too. But not unbelievable for Sunrise. "I don't have a job in Dallas or anywhere else."

His jaw dropped. "You don't?"

She shook her head. "Lance's housekeeper misinterpreted his meaning when he told her he was certain I'd take a job in a top restaurant in Dallas instead of staying here too long."

"Wow. Les Tucker was so sure you were leaving. I'm sorry. I was wrong not to ask you if the rumors were true."

"It's okay. The truth is out now." Part of the truth. She still loved the man standing too close to her, but she didn't dare tell him that.

"Not the whole truth." He looked straight into her eyes.

"What do you mean?"

"None of what I need to say is easy. I'd be more comfortable on horseback riding through some of my favorite spots. Please?"

"Okay." He wasn't the only one with a dry mouth now.

After being sure she was comfortable on the same horse she'd ridden the first time, he swung up into his saddle. He guided his horse away from the barnyard. Rachel followed.

He said nothing until he halted his horse at the top of a ridge. "Looking down at the pasture is one of my favorite things to do. Especially in spring when the wildflowers are blooming and it looks like one of the quilts my grandmother made."

The green grass dotted with mesquites and black cows was an idyllic sight. She shouldn't be here gazing at another inspiring place she'd soon have to forget.

He sucked in a deep, ragged-sounding breath. She twisted in her saddle to look at him.

"Gabe's not the only one who owes you an apology."

"Really?" She gripped the reins.

"I came into the kitchen yesterday while Aunt Sharon was using the mixer. She couldn't hear a word I said until I talked loud enough to be heard. Forgive me for insisting you should have heard Gabe and Peanut go out the door."

"I forgive you." The words came out more easily than she'd thought they would when she'd wished he'd admit how wrong he'd been. Maybe because her heart had never stopped wishing to hear such words.

A broad smile spread across his face. "Thanks." The smile disappeared as quickly as it had started. He stared ahead toward the pasture. "I was so hard on you because I assumed you were like Gabe's mother. Would abandon him the way she did, especially after I heard about the Dallas job."

"I don't understand." The pained look in his eyes made her want to understand. To find a way to keep him from hurting.

"She got tired of this place. Tired of marriage. Tired of Gabe. I couldn't let that happen again. Especially not to Gabe." His voice cracked. "My story's a little long, but you deserve to hear the whole thing."

"Okay…"

"Alicia always loved doing plays in high school. When a movie company came to Sunrise, they hired her as an extra. The director took an interest in her for more than her talent and promised to make her a star. Alicia left for California with him."

"Oh, Mac. I'm so sorry."

"So am I. I assumed you'd never be happy here. That you'd go back to Dallas as soon as you could."

Absorbing everything he'd said left her with no words to reply as he continued to study her.

"All that doesn't excuse the way I hurt you. I'm sorry."

"I know what it's like to be lied to and hurt. That's why I haven't tried to talk to you." She watched a hawk soaring over their heads before turning to look at him again. "Since I misjudged one man, I assumed I'd made another mistake trusting you."

"The way I've been acting, I can't blame you."

"My former fiancé never apologized for what he did to me."

"What did he do?"

She told him about the night her former boss—and fiancé—had broken off their engagement, saying he and his old girlfriend were getting back together. "He even had the nerve to ask me if I'd think about continuing to work for him."

"Wow. But you agreed to something similar when you came to work here."

"Yes, but it was temporary, and I was determined to keep it strictly business between us."

He searched her face. "So are we still strictly business?"

Her heart pounded as she studied him. Her old fears of reading someone wrong fought with the hope his apology and confession had stirred deep within her.

"Maybe I shouldn't have asked that yet." He looked toward the distant horizon. "Can we ride to another favorite place of mine?"

"Okay." She needed time to think and pray. To take in everything he'd said.

Half an hour later, they halted the horses by the path heading down to Longhorn Creek. "Since this is the longest ride you've ever been on, want to dismount and walk to the creek?"

The bench overlooking the peaceful, babbling creek had become one of her favorite places, too. Had Mac figured that out?

"I need to tell you something else." He dismounted his horse, then held out his hands. "I'll help you if you'd like. Or stand here and be sure you don't lose your balance."

"Just stand there." The urge to take a misstep on purpose and end up in his arms again almost overwhelmed her. But she had to be sure this time.

They walked side by side down the path to the creek. "Can we stand or walk since we've been riding awhile?"

"I don't mind." Standing next to him enjoying the tranquil view of the creek felt natural. Right.

He ran the hand closest to her up and down his leg. Was he thinking of reaching for her hand? "So the one more thing I need to tell you is how badly you scare me. My heart is beating so fast I'm amazed you can't hear it."

"I scare you?" She couldn't imagine Mac being afraid of anything.

"More than any coyote, snake or scorpion scares you."

"They don't scare me as bad as they used to."

"Right. Maybe *terrify* is a better word." He reached down for a rock, then skipped it across the water.

"Really? Why?"

"Nothing here can compete with Dallas. With where you want to be. Where I don't want to be. Ever."

Clear water ran over rocks glinting in the light of the evening sun. A cardinal sang nearby. She closed her eyes as she breathed in the fresh air. "You've got it wrong, Mac. Dallas can't possibly compete with here."

"You mean that?" His tender gaze spoke to her heart.

She turned to look at him better. His black hat and denim jacket looked nothing like what most people wore in Dallas. The man himself was nothing like the men she'd dealt with known there. "Shopping centers, museums, even specialty grocery stores are overrated compared to sunsets on Longhorn Creek, shooting stars or rolling hills dotted with cows." She almost added, *compared to you.*

"Would you stay here? In Sunrise?"

"Do you want me to?"

He knelt in front of her. "Would forever work for you?"

Her eyes lit up. "Forever?"

His beaming smile filled his face. "Forever. With me. Because I love you."

"Oh, Mac. I love you, too."

He stood, then pulled her close and kissed her. He stepped back and caressed her cheek. "I don't plan on ever apologizing again for kissing you."

"You'd better not." She wrapped her arms around his neck and kissed him back.

He smiled into her eyes. "Let's watch the scenery awhile." He took her hand and led her to the center bench.

"Won't your aunt and Gabe be back soon?" They might already be wondering where she and Mac had gone.

"Don't worry. After you said you'd go for a ride, I texted her to tell her we might not be around when they came home."

Then he crooked his finger under her chin and lifted her face to kiss her again. "I could get used to watching the creek like this for the rest of my life."

"So could I."

Epilogue

Mac slowed the Mustang as he drove by the weathered sign for Sunrise. "No use letting the local cop ruin the last day of our honeymoon."

"Or our first day back in Hill Country." Rachel looked over at her husband. Her cowboy, back in his usual hat, jeans and boots. Back where he belonged.

Where she now belonged, too. Wearing her jeans and cotton shirt. She'd worn hers for other reasons. Mac would find out why once they reached the ranch.

"Want to stop and say hi to Miss Connie? I mean, Granna."

"No, I'm sure she's fine."

Mac laughed. "Yeah, I'm sure she is. But I don't mind saying hi to Granna for a minute if you'd like."

"I'd rather go home first."

The light turned green. When they drove past Tucker's Farm and Ranch Supply, Les paused from cleaning his store window and waved. They waved back.

"I might learn my way around that store now."

Mac nodded. "You will. We'll have to go in and get you a good pair of boots for riding. And a cowboy hat."

His words warmed her through and through. Her own boots and hat. Maybe more jeans, too.

They drove west, out of town. Rachel drank in the hills and valleys. The farmers' freshly plowed fields, ready for spring planting. Cows grazing behind fences. They'd be at their ranch in another thirty minutes.

Mac turned the car onto the ranch road. She now knew where it curved, where she could catch her first glimpse of the wooden arch that marked the entrance to the ranch.

"Stop when you get to the gate."

"Why?" Mac looked over at her.

"I want some pictures."

"You've taken enough photos the last week to do us for a year. We've got seagulls, waves, sunsets on the beach and everything else around the Florida Keys."

He slowed as they approached the arch.

"Stop here," she said. "I don't want the car in any of the shots."

"Yes, ma'am." He tipped his white straw hat to her.

Rachel grabbed her good camera from the back seat.

"I want one of the two of us standing on the road in the middle of the arch and the wagon wheels on each side of the posts. I'll take a close-up of the sign hanging down with the name of the ranch. A close-up of us by one of the wheels and—"

"And we'll still be here tomorrow. What are you going to do with all those pictures?"

"I want to make a collage." She checked the lighting on her camera. "We'll get the one with the arch and sign hanging down first. I'll set the delay timer so I can come stand by you."

Her husband stood and posed wherever she asked for the next half hour. Without too many complaints. "This is the last one?"

"Not quite." She set her camera on top of the car, then pulled her phone out of the pocket of her jeans.

"What are you doing?"

"Asking your parents to bring Gabe here. I texted them yesterday and asked if they could have Gabe in his good jeans and ready for pictures around this time."

"More pictures?"

"Yes. Family pictures. Of the three of us and the five of us. Peanut, too."

He leaned against the car. "Why are you doing this?"

"Because this is our first time coming home as husband and wife." She slipped her phone in her pocket. "Because the first time I came here, I was looking for home in the wrong place. I found it here at Still Waters."

"Guess that's a good enough reason for taking a hundred pictures." He took her in his arms and kissed her. He traced her cheek with his finger. "You realize a five-and-a-half-year-old boy won't stand still for twenty pictures."

"Yes. But the promise of chocolate chip cookies tomorrow should be a good bribe."

Mac laughed.

Rodger and Caroline, in their truck, soon parked next to the Mustang. Gabe scrambled out of the pickup.

"Daddy. Miss Rachel." He hugged Mac, then Rachel.

Mac patted his son's head as his dad lifted Peanut from the back seat.

He cocked his head Rachel's direction. "I'm still trying to decide your name now."

"Like I said before, you don't have to rush." Gabe had been thrilled when his father and Rachel told him they were going to marry. Getting used to so many changes would take time. She'd be happy with whatever he chose to call her.

"Okay, buddy. Pictures. Lots of pictures." His dad grinned at Rachel.

Gabe grimaced.

"I'll make you chocolate chip cookies tomorrow. You can have one in each hand." Rachel hoped her idea would work. For a few minutes at least.

"Yippee!"

About twenty minutes later, Rachel finished setting up the camera for the last shot of her, Gabe and Mac together. The one with them standing in front of the wagon wheel.

"That was the last one. You've earned a whole bunch of cookies, little guy. You did great." She bent to hug Gabe.

He took a step back. The serious look in his eyes made her wonder if they'd taken too many pictures. "Know what I want to call you?"

"What?"

"Mama. Can I call you that?"

"Oh, yes. I would love to be your mama."

He wrapped his arms around her neck. "I finally gots a mama. I've wanted one so bad."

Mac knelt beside them and engulfed them both in his arms, then kissed Rachel's cheek. "We all got what we wanted."

* * * * *

Dear Reader,

Thank you so much for choosing *A Mother for His Son*! I enjoyed bringing Rachel and Mac to life, as well as Mac's son, Gabe. I hope they'll become your new friends, too.

I've always loved the Texas Hill Country, so setting up my make-believe town of Sunrise there was fun. I have fond memories of visiting the area since I was a child. If you get a chance to see the spring wildflowers there, don't miss it. I hope and pray you've got your own piece of peace like Still Waters Ranch. Finding a home like that is priceless.

Again, thank so much for picking up my book. Please go to bettywoodsbooks.com for my information about me. I'd love to hear from you!

Betty Woods

LOVE INSPIRED

Stories to uplift and inspire

Fall in love with Love Inspired—
inspirational and uplifting stories of faith
and hope. Find strength and comfort in
the bonds of friendship and community.
Revel in the warmth of possibility and the
promise of new beginnings.

Sign up for the Love Inspired newsletter
at **LoveInspired.com** to be the first
to find out about upcoming titles,
special promotions and exclusive content.

CONNECT WITH US AT:

f Facebook.com/LoveInspiredBooks

🐦 Twitter.com/LoveInspiredBks

COMING NEXT MONTH FROM
Love Inspired

HER FORBIDDEN AMISH CHILD
Secret Amish Babies • by Leigh Bale

Four years after bearing a child out of wedlock, Tessa Miller is determined to provide for her son—even if it means working at the diner run by her ex-fiancé, Caleb Yoder. Yet revealing the truth about her past could be the key to the reunion she's never stopped wanting...

FINDING HER AMISH HOME
by Pamela Desmond Wright

After her sister's death, Maddie Baum flees to Wisconsin Amish country with her nephew to protect him from his criminal father. But can she keep the secret from handsome Amish shopkeeper Abram Mueller, who might be the chance at happiness she's been waiting for?

AN UNLIKELY ALLIANCE
K-9 Companions • by Toni Shiloh

With her emotional support dog at her side, Jalissa Tucker will do whatever it takes to ensure the survival of the local animal rescue—even ally herself with her nemesis, firefighter Jeremy Rider. As working together dredges up old hurts, putting the past aside could be the key to their future joy...

A PLACE TO HEAL
by Allie Pleiter

Opening a camp for children who've dealt with tragedy is former police detective Dana Preston's goal in life. And she's found the perfect location—Mason Avery's land. But convincing the widowed dad—and the town—to agree might take a little prayer and a lot of hard work...

THE SOLDIER'S BABY PROMISE
by Gabrielle Meyer

Resolved to keep his promise, Lieutenant Nate Marshall returns to Timber Falls to look after his first love—and the widow of his best friend, who was killed in action. Grieving mom Adley Wilson is overwhelmed by her bee farm and her new baby, and accepting Nate's help may just be the lifeline she needs...

THE TWINS' ALASKAN ADVENTURE
Home to Hearts Bay • by Heidi McCahan

When Tate Adams returns to Hearts Bay, Alaska, for the summer with his adorable twins in tow, Eliana Madden is determined not to fall in love with him again. But she can't refuse when he asks for her help caring for his preschoolers. Could this be the start of a new adventure for them all?

LICNM0522

Get 4 FREE REWARDS!

We'll send you 2 FREE Books plus <u>2 FREE</u> Mystery Gifts.

FREE Value Over **$20**

Both the **Love Inspired®** and **Love Inspired® Suspense** series feature compelling novels filled with inspirational romance, faith, forgiveness, and hope.

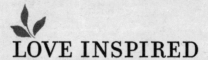